a girl named Nina

Norma Tamayo

This book is dedicated to my father, the love of my life. Papi, I hope I made you proud. Te quiero mucho! And my mother, Mami—te quiero mucho! And my sons, Cesar Jr. and Michael—I wouldn't know what life would be without you guys. I love you both very much. And finally, my husband, Cesar Sr., for putting up with me during my stressful moments. Love you too.

Acknowledgements

I would like to thank Sharon Wells Wagner, my publisher, for believing in me and encouraging me to write. I am so glad that I met you.

I would also like to thank Steve Wagner, Sharon's son, who assisted with publishing my book and created the beautiful book cover.

Thank you to my wonderful friends and family, especially brothers Robert, Jose and Johnny and sister, Lillian who supported and believed in me.

Thank you to my wonderful daughter-in-law, Becky, for giving me a beautiful grandson. CJ—I will always love you.

Many thanks to my wonderful students, former and current, for being my biggest fans.

Prologue

They say that life experiences mold us into the kind of people we are today. I believe that I am who I am today because of what I have been through in my life. I believe that part of me was created by what I witnessed as a child. I also believe that no matter what happens in life, how a person reacts to the situations to which they were subjected, and how they conduct themselves in the future is what makes them who they are today—despite and/or because of what life throws their way.

Part One

1

Lynch Street.
Brooklyn, New York. 1965.

I am Nina. My parents immigrated to New York City from Puerto Rico in 1959, searching for a better way of life for themselves and my brother Bobby. Jobs were scarce on the island. Papi repaired furniture at a furniture store and sometimes worked cutting sugar cane at a local plantation. He worked anywhere he could just to make ends meet, but finding a stable job in Puerto Rico was very difficult. Mami stayed home and made dresses for her neighbors and friends using a hand-cranked sewing machine. No matter how hard they worked, my parents' income was too meager for our family to survive. Although their love for the island would always be felt deep down in their hearts, Mami and Papi both agreed that moving from Puerto Rico to New York City was a necessity in order for their family to thrive.

Upon arriving in New York City, they settled in the Williamsburg section of Brooklyn. There they rented a furnished apartment on Lynch Street. I was born a year later in Saint Vincent's Hospital, located in the Manhattan neighborhood of Greenwich in New York City. According to my father, they were eating dinner in our apartment in Brooklyn with my three-year-old brother Bobby and my grandmother when Mami went into labor. Papi borrowed a neighbor's car and took Mami to the hospital. How my mother managed to give birth to me in Manhattan traveling all the way from Brooklyn is still a mystery to me. It seemed so far away for a woman in active labor to ride in a car, cross over the Williamsburg Bridge, and arrive at Saint Vincent's.

Six years later, in 1965, we were still living in our cramped four-room apartment. A hop, skip, and a jump was all it took to travel from one room to another. The rooms were small and narrow. Bobby and I slept on the sofas in the living room. We had to walk through the living room to get to my parents' bedroom, which was one of two private rooms. The other private room was the toilet room located near the kitchen. We entered our first floor apartment through the kitchen.

Our bathtub, too big for the toilet room, was conveniently located in the kitchen next to the radiator. With only cold water running in our tub, Mami had to heat the water in a large pot on the stove and then empty it directly into the bathtub during our baths. Thank goodness for the shower curtain that gave us privacy. Whenever I took a bath, I made sure that I closed the white plastic curtain all the way. If I'd hear the slightest noise in the kitchen, I would pull my knees together and wrap my hands around my body. *Nobody was going to see me naked,* I thought.

~

Living in a first floor apartment provided us with an interesting view of Lynch Street and Broadway Avenue from our front windows. I could hear people of all colors walking up and down my block just talking and laughing. One day, I saw a brown man with kinky hair (an afro is what Mami called it) holding two wooden sticks under his armpits as he dragged his right leg. A hard, white sock, or maybe even toilet paper, covered the leg. It looked like a mummy's leg, and heavy too! I saw names written all over it. *Wow*, I thought. I had never seen anything like that.

The abandoned building across the street was also interesting to look at. It was covered with big, bright colorful letters and artwork painted by people from the neighborhood. *P-E-A-C-E* and some other letters really caught my attention. I always wondered how people could paint letters that big on a wall.

From my window I could see the underside of the New York City subway, which ran on elevated tracks over Broadway Avenue and intersected with my street. The rattling of the tracks, the brakes squealing, and the horn blowing were the typical noises that woke me in the middle of the night, even with our windows closed. Fascinated by the trains, I would run to the window every time I heard one go by.

"Mami, there it is again," I would say, jumping up and down.

"Okay hija, I heard you," Mami said as she tried to sleep.

~

We typically kept our windows open in the summertime, but one sweltering evening in August changed everything. A five-day heat wave had taken its toll on us and now, immediately after my bath, sweat was already pouring down my forehead. Wearing only a T-shirt and panties, I decided to walk to the kitchen and get a glass of water before going to bed. As I stepped into the kitchen, I noticed that not only was the window open, but the curtains were moving. I didn't feel any air coming in, though.

Suddenly I saw a hand on the windowsill. Then I saw two hands. When I looked closely, I realized that someone was trying to climb into the room. A dark-haired man looked at me, put a finger to his mouth, and muttered, "Be quiet," as he tried to make his way into the apartment.

I turned white as a ghost and my legs began to shake. I could feel my heartbeat racing. I had never seen that man before.

"Mami! Papi! Maaa—mi!" I yelled in my shrill voice.

Within seconds, Mami was by my side. By now the intruder had one foot through the window. Mami began to breathe heavily. I could see her nostrils flare as her face turned red. She didn't waste any time; she grabbed the broom and immediately began to beat on the intruder's body, pushing him back out the window. She beat his head, arms, and legs.

"Get out of my house!" Mami screamed as she pounded

him repeatedly with the broom.

I listened as the intruder begged my mother to stop, shielding himself from my mother's broomstick. I knew that the man had made a big mistake coming here. *Nuh-uh! No way!* Mami was not going to put up with that. In a matter of seconds, the intruder took off. Mami closed the window and locked it. She took a deep breath and turned to me, her face completely relaxed.

"Are you okay Nina?" she asked.

I nodded my head and quickly hugged my mother.

"He left and will never come back," she said.

Mami hugged me back. She carried me to the sofa. My pillow and blanket were already laid out. She tucked me in and kissed my forehead.

"Bendición Mami," I said.

"Dios te bendiga hija," Mami said. "Good night, Nina."

A sense of pride came over me. After all, my mother had saved my life. I had always sensed that my mother was strong. Physically she was big-boned and emotionally she was tough. Mami was a pretty woman with a creamy complexion and short, dark hair. At five feet, two inches tall, she weighed about 150 pounds. She had the tiniest waist. People always commented on her figure. "You have a guitar-shaped figure," they would say.

I knew that my mother, Lydia Tavarez, would always protect me. Her strong family bonds made her very protective of Bobby and me. As the fifth child of eleven, Mami had learned how to stand up for herself. Assertive and never holding any-thing back, Mami was not afraid of anything. She knew how to defend herself even with the limited English that she spoke.

This night there were just the two of us in the apartment; my father was at work. Mami didn't even call my father or the police to tell them about the intruder. How could she anyway? We didn't have a telephone in the apartment. We could not afford one.

My father, Manuel Tavarez, worked evening shift at the electronic company that he so worshipped. It was his first real job since the move from Puerto Rico. The job was stable and provided a lot of on-the-job training. Papi was always work-ing. A little different from Mami, Papi was more gentle, kind, and very considerate. An orphan by the age of twelve who was raised by a kind woman in the same neighborhood where he was born, Añasco, Puerto Rico, Papi learned to value and ap-preciate family. I guess this is why Bobby and I meant so much to him. To me, Papi was much more affectionate than Mami. And I loved him. He was my knight in shining armor—and very handsome too. Papi had light skin and light brown eyes. His short dark hair and mustache reminded people of Clark Gable. I heard a woman tell him that one day. He was taller than Mami by a few inches and skinnier than she by a couple of pounds.

The next morning, I awoke to the aroma of fresh coffee, "Hmm! Café Bustelo," I said. Although I was only five at the time, I loved café con leche. Practically all Puerto Rican kids drank coffee at an early age. I loved dipping saltine crackers into my coffee. It was Saturday and that meant Papi was home. I could hear him talking in the kitchen.

"What? Is Nina all right?" he asked after Mami told him about the intruder who had tried to break into the apartment during the night.

"I don't care how hot it gets in here; you have to keep the windows closed at night! It's time for us to move," he said. "We need a bigger apartment anyway, and one that's not on the first floor."

At the sound of Papi's voice, I jumped out of bed, ran to the kitchen, and with a wide grin shouted, "Papi, Papi."

Papi picked me up and gave me a big hug. He kissed me on my forehead.

"¿Como esta mi hija?" Papi asked.

I gave him a kiss on the cheek. "I'm fine, Papi."

I always felt like a princess around Papi; after all, I was daddy's little girl. He made me feel special. Papi made me my favorite mortadella sandwich—Italian bread with slices of Italian sausage and cheese—which was popular in Brooklyn and a Saturday morning tradition here in my house.

"I made you breakfast," Papi said.

"Thank you, Papi," I said.

As I sat down to drink my coffee I heard a knock on the door. Mami opened the door. My brother Bobby had just spent the night upstairs in my grandma's apartment. We called our grandmother Mamá; everyone did. She was my mother's mother. Heavier than my mother, but the same height, Mamá had a head full of white hair and a light creamy complexion with just a few lines around her eyes and forehead. She had a nice smile, but everyone knew that behind that smile was a tough woman, just like my Mami. Bobby was her favorite grandchild. They loved spending time together. Bobby must have smelled Mami's coffee in the hallway.

"How's Mamá doing?" Mami asked.

"She's doing good. I'm hungry!" Bobby said. "Ready to eat."

Bobby was kind of cute, with black hair, slanted eyes, round face, and a creamy complexion, just like *Mami*. He was taller than me and had a big belly. Not wasting any time, Bobby grabbed a chair and sat down to eat. He took a quick bite of his sandwich before anyone else did. I rolled my eyes when I saw how quickly he chewed his food. *He doesn't even stop to breathe, I thought.* Shaking my head, all I could think about was how chubby he was.

~

After breakfast, Bobby went to the kitchen to take a bath in the tub. Papi was ready to spend some quality time with me. He grabbed his newspapers and sat on the sofa.

"Nina, let's read the newspapers," Papi said.

I knew what that meant. I happily sat next to my father. He wanted to teach me how to read. He wanted me to read an article from the *New York Daily News*. Papi tried hard to show me that he could read English, and he did, but with a big Spanish accent. He wanted to impress me, but more importantly, he wanted me to be fluent in the English language.

Papi began to read the cover page: "Mets amaze Dodgers, 7–5." Baseball was the number one sport in Puerto Rico and Papi really liked the sport. Loyal to New York City, Papi preferred the Mets and Yankees to any other baseball team in the country. No wonder he'd saved the two-day-old paper. He turned the page and asked me to read the rest of the article.

"Okay, Nina, read this part," Papi said.

"Li-ttle league cat-cher ex-tends…" I began to read. "Papi, I don't know how to say this one."

"Tra-di-tion-al," he read as he struggled to pronounce the word.

"Oh, okay, tradi-tional," I said a little faster than he did.

"Muy Bien, Nina," he praised me.

Not only did I read the entire article, I actually made sense of it. Papi always thought that I was brilliant. He complimented me all the time, especially after reading an article.

As soon as we finished reading the *Daily News*, Papi pulled out *El Diario La Prensa*, the largest Spanish newspaper in New York. Now I had to read an article in Spanish.

"Luis Muñoz Marin, primer go-be-nador de Puerto Rico…" I read.

"What does that mean?" Papi asked.

"I think he was the first famous person in Puerto Rico," I guessed.

"No, he was the first governor in Puerto Rico," Papi said. Papi was determined to make me bilingual in English and Spanish. He felt the urgency to do this because he wanted me to start kindergarten in September, which was just one month away. Always happy to make him proud, I never minded reading with my father.

After my reading session, and still in my pajamas, I sat in front of the little black-and-white TV in the living room to watch my favorite cartoon, *"Tennessee Tuxedo."* I always found something amusing about the penguin and his best friend, Chumley the Walrus.

"Nina, get dressed after the show is over," Mami said. "We have to go out."

"Okay, Mami," I answered.

Once the cartoon was over, I changed into my polka dot, sleeveless shirt and solid blue shorts. I put on my sneakers and, taking the laces in my hands, made a loop with one lace and wrapped the other around it. I pulled a loop through the middle and there it was, two bunny ears, nice and tight. I felt so proud of myself.

2

A New Apartment

"Apurate Nina, let's go shopping," Mami said.

I hurried as fast as I could. I enjoyed going grocery shopping with my parents and Bobby. We stepped out of the apartment building into the blazing sun. The heat radiated from the streets and I could feel it burning my skin. Papi and Mami held hands like lovebirds as they walked. I walked by Papi's side. Bobby walked behind us, as though he didn't want to be seen with us.

We crossed the street onto Union Avenue and then walked right up to Broadway Avenue. I could see the grocery store from the corner of Union and Broadway. I was a little confused though. Instead of taking a right toward the store, my parents kept walking straight on Union Avenue.

"Mami, where are we going? I asked. "The grocery store is over there."

"We are going to look at some apartments before grocery shopping," I heard my father say.

"Okay Papi," I said.

I had heard their conversation this morning in the kitchen.

I knew that they wanted to move. I didn't mind moving, though. There weren't that many kids around my block on Lynch Street. It was kind of boring where we lived.

I tried to read the street signs as we walked. "Union Avenue, South 2nd Street?" I asked.

"Yes, hija," my father responded with a smile on his face. He loved the fact that I always tried to read the street signs or anything that came into view.

"My daughter is so smart!" I heard him say to Mami.

Bobby looked at me and gave me a dirty look. It bothered him when my father said nice things to me. Mami always said more nice things to him than me, anyway. I quickly stuck my tongue out at Bobby and kept walking as I grabbed my father's hand.

We approached South 2nd Street. I could see kids playing on the street—lots of them. A fire hydrant gushed tons of water onto the pavement. Residents typically sought comfort from the heat by opening the fire hydrants. Kids were getting wet as their parents watched them. The water was coming out strong. It knocked a kid on his bottom. Everyone laughed. It looked like fun. *I can't wait to try that,* I thought. I saw some kids sitting on their stoop eating ice cream from the ice cream truck and drinking bottles of soda. Sweat rolled off their foreheads like liquid beads.

After several stops at different apartment buildings on the same street, I realized that my parents were serious about getting a new apartment. They viewed three apartments and before long, they had eyes on an apartment on 385 South 2nd Street. It was a two-bedroom apartment with a living room, kitchen, and private bathroom. There was something special about this apartment. I was so impressed.

This fourth floor, L-shaped apartment had a nice kitchen and living room. I liked that the bathtub was not in the kitchen like in our Lynch Street apartment. Here the bathtub and toilet were in the same room. The kitchen had a nice window which faced the concrete back yard. This apartment had two private bedrooms with windows. The window in the small bedroom faced the back side of the building. From this viewpoint, I could see into the kitchen window and the neighbors' kitchen window right below ours. The window in the big bedroom faced the street and had a fire escape.

"Mami, I like this apartment," I said.

"Bueno," she replied.

I ran to the window in the big bedroom and climbed onto the fire escape. I could see kids everywhere. South 2nd Street was *alive*. There were people standing on the street corners just talking. Some kids sat on their stoops, like people sit on bleachers at a game, as they watched other kids play. Many kids played on the street.

I was amazed to see that there were fire escapes on practically every apartment window. Teenagers and kids were sitting on their fire escapes, just hanging out and listening to music. I could hear a song playing. I closed my eyes as I listened to the soothing lyrics of that song, *"What can make me feel this way?*

My girl (my girl, my girl) Talkin' 'bout my girl (my girl)."

"Wow!" I said.

I went back inside and stood on my tiptoes as I continued to look out the window. Leaning forward on the windowsill, I held my chin with both hands and began to daydream about my family living here. I let my mind wander. I imagined myself here, surrounded by new friends. I could see myself sitting on the fire escape talking to everyone. I could see myself playing games on the street. *This is where I belong*, I thought. All of a sudden, I felt someone put their hand on my shoulder. I turned around and saw Mami standing behind me.

"Let's go downstairs, Nina," she said.

Bobby and I followed my parents down the stairs. When we approached the ground floor, Papi walked over to one of the apartments and knocked on the door. A bald, light-skinned Hispanic man with a mustache came out. I listened as my parents spoke with him. "El Súper," I thought his name was.

"Here is the deposit for the apartment," Papi said. "We would like to move in by the first of the month."

I watched as my father gave El Súper some money.

El Súper replied, "Si señor, whenever you want."

"I want the apartment cleaned up before we move in," Mami told the man in Spanish.

"Si señora, real fast," El Súper said.

We left the apartment building and began to walk back toward Lynch Street.

"Aren't we going grocery shopping?" I asked.

"Yes, stupid, don't you see we are going that way?" Bobby teased.

"Bobby, don't call your sister stupid; she is not stupid," Papi said.

I looked at Bobby with a smirk on my face. "Ha-ha," I whispered. I saw the expression on Bobby's face: *if looks could kill.*

~

We stopped at the bodega. The grocery store was smaller than a supermarket but had lots of Spanish food everywhere. It even had a carniceria. I always got a little grossed out whenever I walked past the meat section. I hated to see raw meat. "Yuck," I would say. My favorite part of the bodega was the front counter. It had shelves filled with all kinds of candy. I loved the Bazooka bubble gum. It came individually wrapped with a Joe comic paper which I tried to read. Cracker Jacks were also my favorite. I loved the prizes inside each box.

"¿Hola, Nina como estas?" The owner asked when I walked in.

"Okay," I said with a smile.

Everyone in the bodega spoke Spanish. They even played Spanish music throughout the store. I liked listening to the music. It reminded me of my father when he sang and played with his band members. I ran to my favorite aisle.

"Hmm, Nestle's Quik," I said. I loved the chocolate powder in my glass of milk; it was so delicious. I grabbed a can and placed it in my parents' cart.

After filling the cart with groceries, my parents decided that they were done shopping. I noticed that the cart was filled to the top and that made me happy. It wasn't often that my parents went grocery shopping. We didn't have a car to take the groceries home, so we had our food delivered to our apartment by the store attendant. My parents stocked up on food as much as they could. And I was glad. I always worried about Bobby going hungry. He liked to eat. Deep down inside, I truly loved my brother, even though he was mean to me most of the time.

My father paid for the groceries. The man behind the register bagged the food and labeled each bag carefully. He knew that he would be the one delivering the groceries to our apartment.

"We'll deliver your groceries within ten minutes. 242 Lynch Street, right?" the man asked my father.

"Yes," Papi nodded.

And just as the store attendant promised, the groceries were delivered to our apartment.

3

385 South 2nd Street.
Brooklyn.

By Saturday, September 4 we had moved into our new apartment at 385 South 2nd Street, apartment number 23. I really liked my new home and the fact that we were still in the Williamsburg section of Brooklyn. I kept repeating the apartment number in my head in order to memorize it. There were so many apartments in this five-story brick building—six on each floor. The floor plan was the same on each level: three apartments faced the front of the building and three faced the rear. My apartment faced the front of the building, which was great because I was able to see all the action in the street. There were no elevated train tracks though—not here. Broadway Avenue was blocks away from our new apartment. We had to walk over to Broadway to see or get on the trains. I wasn't going to miss the noise, anyway. The fire escape and the kids in the neighborhood were good enough for me.

Inside the apartment, Mami and Papi worked fast to set up the new bedroom furniture in their big bedroom. Their large bed looked so comfortable. They had nice white dressers and a large mirror. I wished this was my room, especially since it had the window with the fire escape. Hoping my bedroom would look the same, I walked over to the smaller bedroom and noticed that a small bed and one dresser took up the entire space. I looked into to the living room and saw a mattress on the floor.

"Mami, why do I have to share my room with Bobby?" I asked. "I want my own room."

"I'm older than you. It's my room," Bobby said.

"No, it's my room!" I began to cry.

Mami kneeled in front of me and held me for a moment. She tried to calm me down. "How about if you sleep on this mattress in the living room for now, and Papi and I will buy you another bed to keep in the living room? What do you think?" she asked, "And we'll also buy you a doll."

"But the mattress is on the floor," I said.

Mami wiped my tears away, hugged me tighter, and gave me a kiss on my forehead.

"Okay, Mami, but I want the doll that talks," I said.

"Está bien, hija," Mami said with a smile.

I smiled back, broke loose from my mother's hug, and ran to my parents' room. I walked to the window and climbed onto the fire escape. I saw kids riding their bikes. Three girls were jumping rope. Two of the girls held one rope in each hand. I heard them singing rhymes as they turned each rope while the third girl jumped. I saw two boys playing marbles on the street. I watched another group of kids playing baseball down the street, and saw how one boy held a broomstick and hit a pink rubber ball. I found it strange that the boy was not using a baseball bat and that the ball did not look like a baseball. Still, I was fascinated by the game. My father was a big fan of baseball and so was I. People always told me that I was a pretty little girl and I believed that, but I always liked playing with boys' stuff too.

"Mami, can I go out to play?" I asked. "I want to play baseball with those kids."

"They're playing stickball, not baseball!" Bobby said.

"Nina, it's getting late. You can go out and play tomorrow," Mami said.

"Maa!" I yelled back.

"Maa nothing!" Mami grabbed me by my arm, "Go take a bath!"

I frowned and took a deep breath. "Okay, Mami!"

I ran into the bathroom and closed the door. As the nice claw-foot tub filled with warm water, I grabbed the pink box of Mr. Bubble and poured it into the bathtub. I loved taking bubble baths. I practically poured the entire box into the tub. I turned off the water when I saw that the bathtub was quickly filling up. There were bubbles everywhere. I quickly got into the tub. The sounds were like music to my ears as I played in the bathtub: *splish, splash, bubble, bubble, pop!*

As soon as I felt the water turning cold, I rinsed and dried myself. I wrapped a towel tightly around my body. Mami always covered herself with a towel after taking a bath. I never saw her without clothes, so I was not about to let anyone see me naked.

"Mami, I'm done," I said.

"Okay hija, here are your clean pajamas," Mami said as she stood outside the bathroom door.

I opened the door and grabbed my pink pajamas. I closed the door as tight as I could. The latch on the door was too high for me to reach so I really couldn't lock it. I changed into my pajamas. Then I overheard my parents arguing. I cracked the door open to see what was going on.

"¿Te vas otra vez? Why do you have to go out every Saturday night?" Mami asked Papi.

"You know I have band practice every Saturday night. Besides, we have a big gig next week. That means extra money for us," Papi said.

Mami crossed her arms, looked at him with a straight face and then rolled her eyes. Papi walked over to Mami. He hugged her and gave her a kiss on the forehead.

"Look, you and the kids can come see me play next week, okay?" he said.

Mami looked into his puppy eyes and kissed him on his lips. She could not resist him. She loved him very much.

"Okay, but don't come home late," she said. "Who's picking you up?"

"My friend Cheo, and he's bringing me back home," Papi said.

Mami nodded with a slight smile. Papi gave her another kiss, quickly picked up his guitar, and began to walk out the door. All of a sudden, he remembered something.

"Nina, Bobby," he said.

He knocked on the bathroom door.

"Nina, are you there?" Papi asked.

"Si Papi," I answered. I opened the door and jumped into his arms. I knew that he would come for me. He always did.

"Mmm... I love you so much!" I said.

"Me too! Te quiero mucho," Papi said.

He walked over to Bobby, who was watching television, and gave him a hug.

"Good night, son," Papi said.

"Good night, Papi."

That night, I slept on the mattress in the living room. I really didn't mind sleeping there. I knew I would be able to see Papi when he got home. I needed to know that he came home safely. I laid there on the mattress and stared at the ceiling. My eyes grew heavy and before long I fell into a deep sleep.

4

The Beating

By eight o'clock in the morning, I was wide awake. My heart started to race a little; I hadn't seen Papi come in last night. I sprung from my mattress and slowly peeked into my parents' bedroom. I saw my father on his side, eyes closed and blowing air through his mouth. I was happy to see that he had made it home safely.

I walked back to my mattress and turned on the television to watch cartoons, and that's when I heard a shrill cry. The scream came from the apartment below mine. It sounded like a kid in pain.

"Stop!" I heard him say.

I ran to Bobby's bedroom window to see what was going on. From where I was standing, I was able to look through my neighbor's kitchen window. A tall, skinny man was standing over a boy about my age. The man held a belt in one hand. With his other hand, the man held the boy's right arm. The man swung his belt, hitting the boy repeatedly. It was nonstop. He didn't care which parts of the boy's body he was hitting, either. The man was like a machine. I could hear the sound of the belt making contact with the boy's skin: *whack, whack, whack!* I saw the boy cry, tears running down his face.

"I won't do it again, Papi. Please stop," the boy begged.

"I told you—I told you not to touch that!" the man yelled as he beat his son.

I watched in disbelief as the father whipped his son over and over again. I could feel my heart pounding in my chest as tears ran down my face.

"Stop already," I yelled, but the man couldn't hear me. *How can anyone do that to a kid?* I thought as I took several breaths.

"What are you looking at?" Bobby asked as he got up from his bed and came to the window.

Bobby heard the screams and immediately he knew what was going on. He had heard sounds like that before when we lived on Lynch Street. Kids got beaten all the time by their parents. I was just too young to remember.

"Stay away from the window and mind your own business!" he yelled.

I looked at Bobby. "But... he is crying. He's hurt," I said.

"Just get away from this window," Bobby said. He walked away and climbed back into bed.

I looked out the window once more and this time the man looked right at me. His face really spooked me, especially his gold front tooth. I gasped in horror at the sight of him.

I quickly dropped to the ground and crawled away from the window. I peeked in my parent's bedroom to see if they were up. I wanted to tell them what I had seen, but Mami and

Papi were still sleeping. Papi had come home late, so I decided not to wake them. I closed the door and began to watch cartoons.

~

My parents woke up around 9:00 a.m. Papi got up first and then Mami.

"Good morning, Nina," Papi said. "Are you okay?" He picked me up and held me in his arms. Mami went into the kitchen to make breakfast.

"I'm okay, Papi. I heard a kid crying," I said. "His father was hitting him with a belt."

"Where? When?" Papi asked.

I jumped out of his arms and ran to the window.

"This morning when I got up," I said. "He was screaming so loud. I saw him through this window." Papi walked over to the window.

"Where, Nina?" Papi asked.

"Down there," I said as I pointed to the kitchen window of the apartment below ours.

"Well, there is no one there right now and I don't hear anything," Papi said.

"Bobby heard it too," I said.

"What are you looking at?" Mami asked.

Papi told Mami what I had said.

"Nina, you need to mind your own business," Mami said.

Papi gave Mami a look that said *don't talk to my daughter that way*, but he didn't say it out loud. He changed the subject instead.

"Okay, Nina. Let's eat now. We have to go to church soon."

"Okay, Papi," I said as I hugged him.

Bobby got up and brushed his teeth. Minutes later, we were all eating breakfast together. Bobby just kept eating and eating. I watched him as he ate his food. *My God, he really loves to eat*, I thought.

Soon after breakfast, I got dressed. We were going to Sunday Mass. I loved wearing my little sailor dress to church. I put on my white, cuffed ankle socks and black patent leather flat shoes. I sat on the floor and fastened the buckles on my shoes without any problems. I jumped on my parents' bed to look in the huge mirror which was attached to the bureau. *Not too skinny and not too fat*, I thought. Just right! I knew I was cute. I brushed my brown wavy hair and smiled. I never really saw anything wrong with me, even though I had the darkest skin color in the family. I liked my light brown skin.

5

Sunday Morning Mass

Mami once said that Transfiguration was one of the most beautiful churches in Brooklyn, and I believed it. It was beautiful. It had high ceilings with a big cross on the wall above the altar. The table on the altar had nice candles. All the windows were rounded at the top and every one of them had artwork of Jesus and his friends. A big bowl filled with holy water sat at the back of the church. Papi had taught me how to bless myself by dipping my fingers in the bowl and making the sign of the cross. We did this every time we entered and left the church.

Mass was scheduled to start at noon. My parents knew that we had to walk several blocks before arriving at Transfiguration Church on Marcy Avenue; therefore we left for church around 11:15 a.m. As we walked toward the corner of the block, I turned around and looked back at my apartment building; something had made me turn around. I saw someone on the fire escape below mine. I recognized him by what he was wearing. He was that little boy who had been badly beaten by his father this morning. The boy looked at me and waved. I waved back. I really felt sorry for him. I kept seeing his image in my head as we walked to church.

I always felt a sense of relief and peace in church. I remembered the year before when we had lived on Lynch Street. It was Christmas time and I overheard my parents arguing about money.

"We can't afford a tree this year. No presents either," Papi said. "We only have enough money to pay the rent and bills."

"I understand," Mami said as she frowned.

Later that evening, as we were eating dinner, Mami looked at Bobby and me and began to explain what would happen on Christmas day.

"Nina, Bobby, we don't know if Santa Claus will be coming here this Christmas," Mami said. Tears filled her eyes.

"Why, Mami?" I asked.

"We don't have money for Christmas presents—I mean a Christmas tree," Mami said. She quickly corrected herself to avoid ruining the whole Santa Claus myth. I noticed how upset Mami was. I was too. I sighed at the thought of Santa Claus not coming to my house.

"That's okay, Mami. We don't need anything," Bobby said.

I looked at Bobby and noticed him winking at me.

"Yeah! That's okay, Mami and Papi. We have each other," I said.

Mami and Papi looked at Bobby and me. I could tell they were proud of us. But deep down inside I felt sad for all of us. *What's a Christmas without presents?* I thought.

A few days later we were in church attending the Christmas Eve mass. I followed my parents' movements as they kneeled, made the sign of the cross, sat down, and listened to the priest speak. As soon as my parents went up to the altar to get the bread, I kneeled in front of the cross and prayed for Santa to come and bring us Christmas presents. After the priest gave us his blessing and right before mass ended, he made an announcement.

"We have Christmas presents for all the kids here today," he said. "Come up to the altar to get your presents."

The kids rushed to the altar to get their presents, including Bobby and me. I smiled as I approached the priest. I almost sat on his lap, but I knew that he wasn't Santa Claus.

"Thank you, Father," I said as he gave me and Bobby our gifts. "But do you have a present for my Mami and Papi too?"

Father looked around the altar and smiled.

"Yes, as a matter of fact I do." Father got up and picked up a pot of red flowers that I always saw in church around Christmas time. He walked up to Bobby and me and said, "Here, give this to your parents."

"Thank you, Father," Bobby and I said at the same time.

"Go in peace," Father said.

Bobby and I ran to Mami and Papi and we gave them the flowers. They looked at us and then at Father. They smiled and nodded as they both said, "Thank you." We were so happy. Everyone got a present. My prayers were answered. *God is good,* I thought.

Today was more important, though. I had to say a prayer for the boy on the fire escape. I approached the pew, kneeled, and made the sign of the cross. I closed my eyes, folded my hands in front of me, and prayed hard. Although I tried to pay attention to the priest as he lectured, I just couldn't get that boy out of my head. I prayed and prayed that he would be all right.

The church was full of people. Just about everyone from Brooklyn came to this Spanish mass, or at least that's what it looked like to me. All of the local Puerto Ricans came here and they seemed to know each other. I saw people who we knew from Lynch Street and some familiar faces from around my new neighborhood.

After mass ended, my parents walked out of church and hung around for a few minutes to talk to their friends. The men shook hands and the women hugged each other. I recognized a lot of them. Many lived on my block. Most of them lived in my apartment building. My parents proudly introduced me and Bobby to their friends.

Within minutes, a man approached Papi. "¿Manuel, como estas?" He asked as he held out his hand to shake hands with my father. Papi smiled and shook his hand. I was shocked. I couldn't believe it. That was him—the mean man who was hitting the boy with the belt. The man with the gold tooth. He extended his hand to my mother to greet her.

"Hola Lydia," he said as he shook my mother's hand.

"Freddy," Papi said, "I would like you to meet my daughter Nina and my son Bobby."

Freddy looked at Bobby and me.

"Pero que lindos son," Freddy said. "They are beautiful."

I looked down and tried to hide behind my father. I couldn't stand the sight of that man. To me, he was creepy and mean.

"What's wrong, Nina? Say hello," Papi said.

I kept my head down, but to please my father, I cracked a fake smile. I couldn't bring myself to look at Freddy. Papi didn't realize that Freddy was the man who was beating his son this morning. Papi continued his conversation with Freddy. I pouted, made a wry face and almost began to cry. *How could you be friends with him?* I thought. I took a deep breath and managed to hold back my tears. I walked away and sat quietly on the front steps of the church. Bobby seemed content as he tried to socialize with the adults.

As I sat on the steps, I stared into the palms of my hands. My chin began to tremble and I immediately covered my face. Feeling deep sadness, I couldn't stop thinking about that poor boy and that mean Freddy! Tears streamed down my face. I was holding my face in my lap when I heard a tiny voice. A little girl, my height with dark, wiry hair, fair skin, and big brown eyes, came up to me. She must have been my age.

"What's your name?" she asked.

I looked up. "Nina. My name is Nina. What's yours?"

"I'm Millie," the little girl said. "My real name is Milagros, but everyone calls me Millie. I think you live in the same building where I live. I saw you in the hallway yesterday. You were going up the stairs."

"What apartment do you live in?" I asked.

"Number 19. I live on the 3rd floor," Millie said.

"Oh, mine is number 23," I said. "I have a fire escape; do you?"

"Yeah, but I can't see the street. I can only see the back yard," Millie said.

"Where's your Mami and Papi?" I asked.

"Right there, talking to your Mami and Papi," Millie said.

I turned around and saw a woman and a man talking to my parents. I had never seen them before. They smiled as they talked. Then I heard my parents saying goodbye to them.

"Nina, let's go," Mami said as she walked toward me.

I looked at Millie. "I have to go now."

"I know," Millie said. "Bye."

"Bye," I said.

~

My parents, Bobby, and I walked back to our apartment. When we approached our building, I looked up to see if the boy was still on the fire escape. *Nope, no boy*, I thought. I tagged behind as my parents and Bobby rushed up the stairs.

Upon approaching the top of the stairs on the third floor, a boy sitting in the hallway with marbles scattered all around him caught my attention. I tilted my head and leaned forward as I tried to get a close look at him. The boy was barefoot and wearing a long sleeve, striped shirt and long pants. He had straight dark hair and light brown skin, the same color as mine. He was very skinny. I noticed a purple mark on his face. *That's him,* I realized. It was the same boy who had been beaten by his father this morning.

His sad, red eyes met mine as he gave me a quick, half-hearted smile. The boy knew that I recognized him. Cheeks blushing, he covered his face with his hands as he pulled his knees together. I began to walk toward him. When he saw me coming, the boy sprang forward, picked up his marbles, and dashed inside his apartment.

"Apartment 17," I whispered. "That's where he lives."

"Nina, hurry up," I heard my brother yell. I heard the sound of my mother's keys as she opened our apartment door.

I ran up the stairs as fast as I could. Upon entering the kitchen, I noticed that Mami already had her apron on and was starting to prepare lunch as Bobby sat at the table. I breezed by them and rushed to the bedroom. Since Bobby and I shared the same closet and dresser, I hurried and changed into my play clothes before Bobby walked into the room.

I put on my favorite navy blue, sleeveless shirt, blue shorts and white, pointy Keds sneakers. I was ready to go outside to play. I looked out my parents' bedroom window and saw kids playing on the sidewalk. Millie and two other girls were playing jump rope in front of the apartment building. She still had her dress on, the one that she wore to church. I saw many kids playing all kinds of street games, but the boys playing stickball really caught my eye. I walked back to the kitchen.

"Mami, can I go out to play now?" I asked.

"Nina, you have to eat first," Mami said.

I chewed my peanut butter and jelly sandwich as fast as I could and drank my glass of chocolate milk.

"All done, Mami," I announced as I began to open the door.

"Stay in front of the house where I can see you," Mami said.

"Okay, Mami," I replied.

6

Strange Encounter

I bounced down the stairs as quickly as I could. On reaching the second floor, a door creaked down the hall and I froze in my tracks. Someone was peeking through a door from one of the rear apartments. It was a boy or a man. I couldn't tell. He looked older than my brother Bobby, but younger than my father. He had a long, narrow face, pitted and scarred. I squinted my eyes as I tried to see who he was without getting too close.

The person was breathing hard with his tongue sticking out. His pants zipper was open and he was holding something in his hand. He motioned to me with his free hand, suggesting that I move closer. It was dark at that end of the hallway; I couldn't really see what he was holding, but he gave me the creeps. I instantly felt chills going down my spine. I turned my head and ran down the stairs. I felt scared, but didn't know why. I thought the man was weird.

I finally made it outside. Distracted and too excited to play, I quickly forgot what I had just seen in the hallway. Millie approached me first. She looked into my eyes, grabbed my hand, and walked me down the stoop.

"Nina, come play with us," she said.

Millie smiled as she introduced me to her friends.

"These are my friends, Sara and Blanca," Millie said.

"Hi," I said. I thought they were both cute. Sara and Blanca were about the same height, a little shorter than Millie and me. Sara was thin with a light complexion, long, light brown hair, and brown eyes. She had such a nice smile. Blanca had more of a round body. She had a big stomach and darker skin, a little darker than mine. Her long, brown hair was tied up in a pony tail. Her eyes were big and dark.

"You want to jump rope with us?" Sara asked.

"I don't know how," I said.

"We'll show you," Sara said.

Millie and I turned the rope as Sara and Blanca jumped in. Then it was my turn to jump with Millie. It didn't take long for me to learn how to jump rope. We used a single rope so it was easy to enter as the rope turned. We jumped until we missed. After several misses, we took a break and sat on the stoop. Sara dug in her pocket, took out a piece of bubble gum, and put it in her mouth. She chewed the bubble gum quickly and within seconds she began blowing bubbles.

"How do you do that?" I asked.

"It's easy," Sara said. "You just put the gum in your mouth, chew it until it's nice and flat, and then roll the gum into a ball—just like this."

Sara stuck out her tongue to show us. Millie, Blanca, and I looked closely.

"Then you move this ball behind your front teeth, make it flat with your tongue, and blow air into it," Sara said. "It takes practice, but it's easy to do."

"Who taught you?" Blanca asked, "Do you have some more?"

"No, I don't. That was my last piece," Sara said. "My mother taught me."

"Do you have any sisters?" I asked.

"Nope, it's me and my three little brothers," Sara said. "Sometimes I have to help my mother take care of them, but it's not too bad."

"Where's your father?" I asked.

"He's always driving a taxi," Sara said.

"I'm glad I don't have to take care of little brothers," Blanca said as she stood up and put her hands on her waist. "I have three big ones and sometimes they are mean to me so I push them."

"Don't they hit you back?" Millie asked.

"Nope, they'd better not or my father will hurt them," Blanca said.

"Wow," I said. "What about you, Millie? Do you have any brothers or sisters?

"Yeah, I have one, " Millie answered. "She's a baby but Mami takes care of her, not me."

"Nina, do you have brothers and sisters?" Sara asked.

"Just one. I have a brother," I said. "He's older than me."

"What apartment do you live in?" Sara asked after popping

her bubble gum.

"Apartment 23, right up there," I said as I pointed at my fire escape.

The girls looked up at the building and nodded. Then Millie picked up the jump rope and we began to jump rope again. We kept talking until we got to know each other some more. As we talked, I found out that Sara and Blanca lived in the same apartment building across the street from mine. Millie, Blanca, and Sara had lived on South 2nd Street since they were born and were friends ever since.

It was my turn to jump when some boys came up to watch us. I recognized them. They were the ones playing stickball down the block. I could tell that the girls knew them too.

"Can I jump in?" asked the one boy.

The girls looked at the boys and gave them dirty looks.

"How come you're not playing stickball?" I asked.

"We need two more players," the one boy said. "Hector and Johnny went home."

"Oh, I'll play," I said.

Millie pouted, "But what about our jump rope game?" She said.

"You can play too!" I said.

"No, that's a boy's game; I don't want to play that," Millie said.

Sara looked at Millie and me.

"I'll play stick ball. I always wanted to learn," Sara said as she looked at me. *She was so much like me,* I thought.

"Me too," Blanca said as she rolled her eyes at Millie. I could tell that she was tough.

Sara, Blanca, and I followed the boys as they walked down the block. Millie walked right behind us. Edwin, the leader, explained the rules. He seemed to know a lot about the game.

"Stickball should really be played on the street," Edwin said. "But I know that some of you are not allowed on the street, so we'll play on the sidewalk. We are going to use this broomstick and pink rubber ball. I'll do all the pitching. Nina, you stand here with the broomstick and I'll throw the ball for you to hit. Sara, you stand here and try to catch the ball if it comes your way. Blanca, you stand there and Millie, you stand over there. My boys, Lefty and Joe, know where to stand."

After a quick practice, Sara and I were ready to play a real game. Before we knew it, we were hitting home runs. We laughed when we tried to throw fast pitches. The ball went everywhere except toward the batter. We were having so much fun.

Several hours had passed when I heard my mother calling my name.

"Nina, come up. It's time to eat!"

I looked up at the fire escape and saw Mami looking out the window.

"Okay, Mami," I said.

I dropped the broomstick and waved goodbye to my friends. I ran up the stoop and opened the big front entrance door. I climbed the stairs as fast as I could. Upon approaching the landing on the second floor, I slowed down and looked around for that creepy person. I took a deep breath. *Good!* I thought. *Nobody around.* I continued to run up the stairs.

I could smell Mami's cooking in the hallway. "Hmm. Arroz con pollo, yellow rice with chicken—delicious!" I said.

I made it up to my apartment and quickly opened the door. Serving dinner as she normally did, Mami stopped to look at me.

"Nina, go wash your hands," she ordered.

"Okay, Mami," I said.

I ran to the bathroom and washed my hands. Bobby and Papi were sitting at the table in the kitchen. I pulled out a chair and sat down. Mami had already served my food. I slathered the rice with ketchup. I loved ketchup. In fact, I put it on practically everything I ate. Mami and Papi continued to talk about their daily routines at work and home. Then they began to talk about school.

"I want Nina to start kindergarten this year," Papi said.

"Manuel, kindergarten is only in the morning. We don't have anyone to pick up Nina at twelve o'clock." Mami said. "Bobby is in school all day. He wouldn't be able to bring her home. I have the opportunity to work as a seamstress and I want to work! We can use the money."

"What would we do with Nina? Who is going to take care of her?" Papi asked. "What about her education, Lydia?"

I picked at my food as I listened to my parents argue. I was never a big eater anyway. Bobby, on the other hand, was already starting his second plate.

"Look, Nina can wait one more year," Mami explained. "Next year she can skip kindergarten and go right to first grade. She is smart. She can do that. Meanwhile, Carmen, la esposa de El Súper, can take care of her. Carmen doesn't work."

Papi was silent for a few seconds. He thought about it. "Nina, hija, how do you feel about not going to school this year?"

"It's okay, Papi. I can still read with you," I said, trying to keep the peace between my parents.

Papi smiled. I was his princess and he only wanted the best for me.

~

Later that evening, Mami, Papi, and I went downstairs to visit Carmen. El Súper opened the door.

"Come in," he said. My parents and I walked in.

"Can we speak with your wife, Carmen?" Papi asked.

"Yes, sure," El Súper said. "Car-men!"

Carmen came to the door. Her eyebrows lifted as she smiled. She was taller and heavier than Mami, with short dark hair, dark eyes, and skin. The bags under her eyes made her look older than Mami.

"May we speak with you?" Papi asked.

"Yes, how can I help you?" Carmen said. "Come in."

We walked through the kitchen and into the living room.

Their apartment looked like ours. It had a nice kitchen, living room, and from what I could see, it had two bedrooms. All the walls were painted white. I noticed a big picture of Carmen and her husband on the wall. No kids though. We sat on the brown sofas as Carmen offered us something to drink.

"¿Café?" Carmen asked.

"No, gracias," Papi answered.

"We just finished eating," Mami said.

"How can I help you?" Carmen said.

"My wife would like to work as a seamstress in a factory on Grand Street, but we need a babysitter. We need someone to take care of Nina while we work," Papi said.

"Yes, Carmen, that's true. I can start tomorrow. They are going to teach me how to make coats," Mami said.

Carmen looked at me and smiled. I smiled back.

"Okay, what time will you bring her?" Carmen asked.

"Around 7:30 in the morning," Mami said.

They just kept talking and talking. Feeling bored, I walked over to the window in the living room. Since Carmen's apartment was located in the rear of the building, I was only able to see the back yard. The ground looked like sidewalks; there was no grass. The entire area was fenced in. Everyone who lived in the rear of the first floor had access to the yard, but there was nobody around. All the kids were probably out front playing. I began to yawn and was now starting to feel tired.

"Okay, thank you Carmen. Let's go Nina," Mami said.

Papi shook hands with El Súper. "We'll see each other

again," he said. "Good night."

We went upstairs to the apartment. I was so tired that I took a quick bath and soon fell fast asleep on the mattress in the living room.

~

Shortly after falling asleep, I was awakened abruptly by the sound of sirens and lights flashing in the street.

At first, I thought that the lights were flashes of lightning. I got up anyway and ran to my parent's bedroom to look out the window. My parents and Bobby were already sitting on the fire escape looking down at a commotion on the street. We watched as a police officer led a man out of my building in hand cuffs. The man kept his head down.

As the officer escorted the man into the police car, the man looked up at us. I gasped in horror at the sight of him. I pulled my head back into the room and held my hand close to my chest. That was him! The man from my strange encounter in the hallway today was being arrested. I walked over to my mattress and laid down without mentioning the man to my parents. I was too scared to say anything. I was also afraid that my parents wouldn't let me go outside to play if I told them what I had seen earlier today.

Thank God, the police got him! I thought.

7

The Babysitter

The next morning, I felt Mami tugging on my shoulder, trying to wake me up. *It's early,* I thought. She was rushing as she helped me get dressed. I sat down to eat the oatmeal that Mami had made me. I watched her run around the apartment looking for her shoes. I could tell she was nervous about starting her new job. I ate as quickly as I could.

"Are you done, Nina?" she asked.

"Yes Mami," I said. I loved to write so I grabbed my little notebook and pencil.

"Let's go," she said.

Mami took me down to the Super's apartment and off to work she went. Bobby had already left for school. Even Papi had gotten an early start to work today. I overheard him tell Mami that he was promoted to a new position at the electronic company and needed to go in for training.

My first day at the babysitter was pretty boring. I didn't know Carmen very well and she didn't have kids, or at least not that I could see. I was quiet the entire day. I watched TV and practiced writing my first name in my notebook as Carmen mopped the floors and dusted the furniture. She wiped her plastic-covered brown sofas with a wet cloth. She reminded me of Mami when she cleaned the house every Saturday morning. Every once in a while Carmen would stop to ask me questions.

"Would you like something to eat, Nina?" she asked. "Can I get you anything?"

"No," I said softly.

Around twelve o'clock, Carmen served me some home-made chicken soup. It was delicious. I could tell that Carmen liked to cook. I could smell her food every day in the hallway just like I did Mami's. Carmen sat down next to me. She told me how much she liked to jump rope when she was a little girl.

"When I was a little girl, I used to jump rope every day with my sister in Puerto Rico," she said with a smile. "I jumped rope faster than anyone in my neighborhood."

I chuckled when she said that. "Where is your sister now?" I asked.

"My sister still lives in Puerto Rico. She likes it there," Carmen said.

"Do you have any kids?" I asked after getting the courage to do so.

"I only have a son, but he doesn't live here. He's all grown up," Carmen said.

We talked for a little while longer. Then Carmen got up, took the dirty dishes to the sink, and wiped the table. I walked back into the living room to watch cartoons as Carmen washed the dishes. I wrote in my little notebook some more. Papi had taught me how to write my name, so I practiced writing it every chance I could. *Nina Inez Tavarez.* I loved the sound of my name. I practiced writing numbers and drew stick figures of my friends and family.

I heard someone knocking on the door around four o'clock. Carmen looked through the peep hole and then opened the door. It was Mami. She had come to pick me up.

"Hola Carmen, hola Nina," Mami said.

"Ma-mi!" I shouted. I was so happy to see her.

"How was your first day of work?" Carmen asked Mami.

"Bien, it was fine," Mami said. "I learned a lot, but it's piece work so I have to be fast."

"Oh, so the more coats you make, the more you get paid, right? Is that how it works?" Carmen asked.

"Si, the foreman will count every coat that I sew and write it down. And then he pays me every Friday," Mami said.

"Muy bien," Carmen said.

"¿Como estas mi hija?" Mami asked as she looked at me.

"Good," I said as I looked at Carmen. "She is very nice."

Mami took my hand. "Gracias, Carmen. I'll see you tomorrow morning."

"Si, I'll see you tomorrow. Adios Nina. You can bring your toys if you want," Carmen said.

"Okay," I said. "Bye, bye."

It didn't take long for me to get used to the babysitter. The routine was the same every weekday: Mami would drop me off and then pick me up when she was done with work. Mami would start dinner and cook for us. Papi always worked late. He never made it home in time to eat dinner with us—not during the week. The nice thing about Mami working was that my parents were able to buy extra things for our apartment. We even got a telephone.

Carmen was really nice. Some days she would take me shopping on Grand Street. We would look at all sorts of household items and clothes, but we always came home empty-handed. Most of the time we went grocery shopping at the bodega across the street.

The bodega had its own deli and typical stuff that a regular grocery store would have. Men would normally hang outside the store playing dice against the brick wall. Carmen knew everyone at the bodega.

"Hola, Carmen, how are you?" Rafael, the store owner, asked as we passed him in the store. "Nina, how are you?"

"We are fine," Carmen answered for both of us.

"Carlos, can I have a pound of cooked ham?" Carmen asked the guy behind the counter.

"Si," Carlos said.

Not only did Carmen know everyone in the bodega, she also knew everyone in the neighborhood, including the parents and kids in our building.

8

Miguel

One day, when Carmen and I were getting back from the bodega, we saw the boy from apartment 17 sitting alone on the stoop. He seemed to be looking for something to do. He watched us as we crossed the street. As we approached the stoop our eyes met and I smiled. I thought he looked better now, not crying like the last time I saw him. He was wearing a blue, long sleeve shirt, black pants, and black sneakers.

"Hola, Miguel," Carmen said to him.

"Hi," I said smiling. I was glad to see him.

"Hi," he said as he looked up and quickly put his head down.

Carmen noticed the big smile on my face. I guess she realized that I needed someone to play with. So she invited him in to play with me.

"Miguel, do you want to come inside and play with Nina?" Carmen asked. "I'm going to make lunch for all of us to eat."

"Okay," Miguel said.

"Do you need to let your mother know?" Carmen asked.

"Yeah, she's upstairs. I'll go up now and let her know,"

Miguel said. "My Papi is working."

"Okay, go up now and let her know," Carmen said.

"Hooray!" I said excitedly.

Miguel ran upstairs. We heard him go inside his apartment as we waited for him in front of Carmen's door. Miguel came back downstairs holding a few marbles in his right hand.

"Let's go inside," Carmen said as she turned the key and opened the door. She walked in first and I followed. Miguel nodded and walked right behind me.

"Go to the living room while I make you a sandwich," Carmen said.

"Okay, Carmen," I said. "Come Miguel."

He smiled as we walked toward the living room. We quickly sat on the sofa where I kept my Jolly Santa coloring book. I picked up the book and asked Miguel to color with me.

"Do you want to color?" I asked.

"Yeah," he said.

"Let's sit on the floor; it will be easier to color," I suggested.

"Okay," Miguel said as he nodded slowly.

We sat on the shiny, green floor and I gave Miguel my coloring book and crayons. Miguel brought his knees up and held the coloring book there. Still holding the marbles in his right hand, he picked up the box of crayons with his left hand.

"You can pick any picture you want," I said as I turned the pages for him. "Then just color."

"Okay," Miguel said. "I like this picture of Santa Claus."

"Oh, yeah, that's nice. Go ahead and color," I said.

Miguel took the red crayon out of the box and began to color Santa's hat. I watched as he colored quickly and outside the lines.

"You have to do it slow," I said. "You can't color outside the lines."

"Oh, okay," Miguel said. He began to draw again, this time much slower.

"Good," I said, giving him my approval. I looked over to his right hand and saw that he was still holding the marbles.

"What do you have in your hand?" I asked.

He looked at his left hand which was holding the crayon. Then he looked at his right hand.

"Oh, these are my marbles," he said.

"Can I see them?" I asked.

"Yeah, sure, here."

I put my hands together and opened them like a cup. Miguel put his marbles in my hands. They were made out of glass and were colorful, like a rainbow in the sky.

"How many are there?" I asked.

"Thirteen," he said as he continued to color. "You can count them."

"One, two, three, four, five, six, seven, eight, nine, ten, eleven, twelve, thirteen. Yep! You are right. Thirteen marbles," I said as I looked closely at each of them. "How do you play with these?"

"I'll show you," Miguel said with a wide grin. He stopped coloring and took the marbles from my hands. He placed them on the floor. "You put eleven marbles in a circle like this," he explained. "You keep one marble and I keep the other. You hold your marble with your pointing finger like this and you push the marble with your thumb like this. You want to shoot your marble and try to hit the marbles in the circle. You get to keep all the marbles that you hit. The player with the most marbles wins the game."

Miguel and I began to play a game of marbles. I had a hard time pushing the marble with my thumb as I tried to hit the others. I laughed when I missed my shots; I didn't care. We were having fun. Miguel was good at playing marbles and it was nice to see him excited.

"Nina, all you have to do is hit the ball like this," Miguel said as he showed me for the tenth time.

"I just can't do it," I said, laughing out loud and making Miguel laugh as well.

Miguel hit every marble he aimed for. He was winning but that didn't bother me one bit. I just wanted to get to know him.

"How old are you?" I asked.

"Five and a half. I'll be six this year," he said.

"That's how old I am," I said. "Do you have any brothers or sisters?"

"No, it's just me."

"Do you want to hang out with me on the fire escape sometime?" I asked.

"Sure," he said, smiling.

"Nina, Miguel, come eat," Carmen said in a loud voice.

"Okay Carmen," I answered as I looked at Miguel.

Miguel and I picked up the marbles. I noticed that he didn't have a pocket. That's why he kept the marbles in his right hand. We walked over to the kitchen.

"Here Miguel, you can put your marbles in this cup until you are done eating," Carmen said.

"Okay," he said as he put his marbles in the cup on the table.

Miguel and I sat down to eat. The ham and cheese sandwiches and glasses of chocolate milk looked delicious. We dug into our sandwiches while Carmen washed the dishes. I kept looking at Miguel as we ate quietly. He noticed me looking.

"What?" he asked.

"Nothing," I said. I wanted to ask him more questions—questions about his father—but I just couldn't. *Not today*, I thought.

We took our time eating our sandwiches and drinking our chocolate milk. Everything tasted really good. We were almost done with our sandwiches when I heard someone shouting in the hallway.

"Miguel!" a woman yelled. "Miguel."

Carmen also heard the shouting. She opened the door to see who it was. She walked out to the hallway and looked up the stairs.

"Miguel!" The woman shouted again. "Carmen, is Miguel there with you?"

"Si senora. I'll get him for you," Carmen said.

Miguel jumped. "It's Mami," he said. "I have to go now."

Miguel finished his sandwich and drank his milk quickly.

"I'll see you tomorrow, maybe," he said while waving to Carmen and me as he walked out the door.

"Bye," I said.

Carmen closed the door and looked at me with a smile on her face.

"Did you have fun today?" she asked.

"Yeah, it was fun. He is nice," I said as I finished my sandwich.

I got up and took the dirty dishes to the sink.

"That's okay Nina, I'll clean up. You can go watch TV now," Carmen said.

"Oh, okay," I said as I turned around to face the table. "Oh, no! Miguel left his marbles here."

"Let's put them in this plastic bag and we can give it to him tomorrow. Is that okay with you, Nina?" Carmen asked.

"Yeah," I said, nodding my head. "Wait! I can give them to him tonight on the fire escape. May I have them please?"

"Okay, Nina, but if you don't see him tonight bring them back tomorrow so that we can take them to him," Carmen said.

"Okay," I said.

Later in the evening, after dinner, I climbed onto the fire escape hoping to see Miguel. I was sitting quietly, thinking about how much fun I'd had at the babysitter's house, playing with my new friend Miguel. *Playing marbles is fun,* I thought. I began to dream about Miguel and me playing together for a long time, when my thoughts were interrupted by the sound of someone opening a window. I looked down below and saw a boy sticking his head out. It was Miguel.

"Miguel," I called out to him.

He looked up with a smile and pulled himself up to his fire escape.

"Hi, Nina," he said.

"I have your marbles. You left them at Carmen's house," I said.

"I'm coming up," Miguel said. He climbed the stairs slowly and sat next to me on my fire escape.

"Here they are," I said, handing him the plastic bag. "Carmen put the marbles in this bag."

"Oh, okay, thanks," he said as he grabbed the bag.

Miguel sat down for a little longer. We looked around the neighborhood and watched people walking down the street and kids playing on the sidewalk. Blanca, Millie, and Sara were playing jump rope. I could have been down there with them, but I really wanted to see Miguel tonight. I just had to give him his marbles back.

"Miguel?"

"Yes, Nina."

"Why do they hit you?"

"I don't know. It's... it's just my father who really hits me and not all the time. Only when he drinks. He hits my mother too! She's really afraid of him."

"It must hurt!" My eyes filled with tears. "He should take

care of you and love you. Just do what he tells you to do so you don't get hurt!"

Miguel turned around and looked at me with a little smile on his face.

"Okay, Nina, I'll try. But sometimes it is hard for me to stay quiet and it's even harder when he hits my Mami. I don't like that. I don't like to see her cry. He is just a mean old man."

"Why don't you come up here when he tries to hit you? My Papi can talk to him."

"I don't know, maybe."

I wanted to give Miguel a hug, but I held back. I didn't want him to think that I liked him as a boyfriend. I just wanted to be friends with him.

"Miguel!" We heard someone shouting from the window below. He stuck his head out the window and looked up at us. It was Miguel's father, Freddy. Freddy looked at us and smiled.

"Hola Nina," he said.

"Hola," I said, forcing myself to smile.

"Miguel, you have to come down to help clean," Freddy said.

"Okay, Papi. Bye Nina," Miguel said as he rushed down the stairs.

"Bye," I said. "Be careful."

I went back inside and noticed that Mami and Papi were watching novelas in the living room. They loved watching soap operas every night.

"I'm going to take a bath now," I said, letting them know

that it was time for me to go to sleep.

"Okay, hija. I'll get your pajamas," Mami said.

"I'll get your mattress ready," Papi added.

I took a quick bath and put on the pajamas that Mami had left on the door knob. When I got out of the bathroom, the television was off and my bed was ready for me to sleep on. I saw Mami and Papi sitting in the kitchen drinking soda. I walked up to Mami and gave her a hug and a kiss. Then I jumped onto Papi's lap and hugged him really tight.

"I love you, Mami and Papi," I said.

"We love you too," Papi said.

"Papi, I was talking to Miguel on the fire escape." I looked into Papi's eyes. "Can you please, please talk to his father so that he doesn't hit Miguel anymore?"

"Nina, that really isn't any of our business," Mami said.

"Hija, for you… I do anything," Papi said. "I will say something to Freddy the next time I see him. But I will be nice, almost like a friend. Okay?"

"Okay," I said, smiling.

I jumped into bed and began thinking about my day with Miguel. *He is so nice,* I thought. I said a little prayer for him, closed my eyes, rolled over on my side, and fell asleep.

Saturday morning came around and I overheard Papi talking to Mami in the kitchen as I was eating my breakfast.

"I'm just going downstairs to talk to Freddy for a few minutes," Papi said as he winked at me.

"Manuel!" Mami said.

"I'll be nice. I won't offend anyone," Papi said.

"Come back right away," Mami said.

Papi came back smiling some time later. I was sitting on the sofa coloring in my book when I heard Papi and Mami talking in the kitchen.

"What did he say?" Mami asked.

"Oh, nothing. It was just man talk," Papi said with a slight smile. "We'll see."

"Tell me, Manuel," Mami said.

Papi looked at Mami. He was quiet for a moment. I could tell that he didn't want to tell her anything, but Mami insisted.

"I told Freddy how nice his son Miguel is and that Nina likes him a lot as a friend," Papi said with a smile. "I asked him to be more gentle with his son."

"And how did he take it?" Mami asked, tilting her head to the side.

"At first he stepped back and looked at me like *who do you think you are?*" Papi said as he got a little more serious. "Then I told him that he needed to calm down before I call immigration and have him deported back to his country."

"What? He's not Puerto Rican?" Mami said, eyes wide open.

"No. He's either from Central or South America, I can't remember," Papi said. "He tries to sound and act like a Puerto Rican so that people think he is one."

"How do you know this?" Mami asked.

"He told me one day after church," Papi said. "He asked me

never to tell anyone. He's afraid he'll get deported."

Smiling again, Papi peeked over to me and winked. "I think he'll take it easy on Miguel now."

9

Daniel

One nice Saturday afternoon, Papi took me to his band practice at Cheo's house on Ellery Street. Papi practiced with his band members every Saturday afternoon. He had a gig practically every Saturday night. I loved to hear my father sing. I always imagined that he was singing his songs to me. "That's my Papi," I would say. "He sings so beauti-ful-ly."

Mami never liked the idea that he was a musician. She saw how women flirted with him when he sang his songs and played his guitar. She didn't like him coming home late either.

Ellery Street was too far away to walk, so we took a taxi there. I liked Ellery Street. All of the apartment buildings on the block looked the same: three story, brownstone row houses. The kids on the block were very nice. There were four boys, Joselito, Pepito, Sammy, and Daniel, who lived above Cheo's second floor apartment; they were especially nice to me.

When the cab arrived at Cheo's apartment building, I saw the boys walking up the stoop. They didn't see me coming out of the taxi. By the time we got upstairs to Cheo's apartment, the boys were already in theirs. The band members said hello to me and high-fived my father. They didn't waste any time. They picked up their instruments and began to warm up right away. I sat on a chair next to a window and drew pictures of my father and his three band members along with their instruments. The guys were all lined up as they would be on stage. Papi, the main singer, held his maracas up close, one higher than the other, and shook them with the rhythm of the music. Depending on the song, Papi would also pick up his guitar and play along with the guys. Felipe, Cheo's brother and the band leader, played the guitar. He looked a lot like my father: dark hair, light skin, same height and weight—no mustache though. He was handsome too. But my Papi was more handsome. The youngest, Cheo, also played the guitar. He looked a little like his brother Felipe, with lighter skin and the same height and weight. David, who was tall, dark and thin, played los timbales and cowbell. He had a nice smile.

The band played a few popular songs from Puerto Rico. Laying a hand over my heart, I took a deep breath as I listened to my father sing one of Puerto Rico's classic songs, "En Mi Viejo San Juan." I got goose bumps each time I heard my father sing, especially that song; he sang it with all his heart. My father once told me that the song was Puerto Rico's second national anthem. People sang "En Mi Viejo San Juan" with the utmost respect to show support and love for the island.

Almost all of the windows in the apartment building were open that afternoon. It was hot outside. Voices in the street caught my attention. It was the sound of kids playing. I looked out the window and noticed some boys playing with bottle caps. Skelsy was the name of the game. Someone had drawn a big square on the street with chalk. Inside the big square were little ones. I watched closely as each boy tried to land his bottle cap in one of those tiny squares. The squares reminded me of hopscotch except that in hopscotch, the boxes were more rectangular.

The boys looked like they were having fun. I could also hear music and people talking everywhere. I heard a woman from upstairs yell at her kids.

"Go outside to play! I have a headache," the woman yelled.

"Okay Mami," the boys said.

I could hear the boys running down the stairs. Boy, they were noisy! When I looked out the window, I saw Joselito, Pepito, and Sammy running out of the building with their skateboards. They looked excited to ride their boards. I noticed that the little boy, Daniel, was missing. I remember seeing him earlier with the other three boys. I wondered where he was. The four of them were always together.

Joselito, Pepito, and Daniel were brothers. Sammy was a cousin who spent a lot of time upstairs. He practically lived there. Daniel was the youngest brother. Curious about Daniel, I opened the door to the apartment to see if he was in the hallway. I heard someone talking. I stepped out, looked down the stairs, and saw Daniel talking to a strange man as he was holding his skateboard. I didn't know who the tall, blond-haired man was, but Daniel seemed comfortable talking to him. The man even knew Daniel's name.

"I have something you like, Daniel," the man said. He was holding a fudgesicle.

Daniel eyes lit up. "Yeah, I like that," he said. "I love chocolate ice cream."

The man looked at him and said, "Come in. I have a lot of them."

Daniel followed the man into his first floor apartment. Next, I heard the sound of the door closing. I went back to Cheo's apartment and looked out the window. I never saw Daniel come out.

I watched as Daniel's two brothers and cousin rode their skateboards. They were having fun. Joselito was the oldest and he was very good at riding his skateboard. He was able to ride his board and do all kinds of tricks. I laughed when Pepito fell. He saw me laughing too. He gave me a dirty look. I covered my mouth to control my laughter and hid inside.

~

Papi was singing again. I turned around in the chair and just sat there listening to my father sing. *He is a star,* I thought. I had no desire to go outside to play. I just sat quietly by the window and kept drawing in my little notebook as I listened to my father sing.

A few hours went by when I heard the boys' mother yell out the window.

"Where's Daniel?" The mother asked the boys.

"We don't know; he's upstairs with you," Joselito responded.

"No, he's not! Look for your little brother," his mother screamed. The desperation in her voice scared the boys and me too.

Daniel's mother knocked on all the doors in the apartment building looking for Daniel and begged everyone to help her find her son. Within a matter of minutes, every person who lived in the neighborhood was out looking for Daniel. My father and his band members stopped their rehearsal to help look for the little boy. It didn't dawn on me to say anything about what I had seen in the hallway. The man who was talking to Daniel seemed very nice. He may have been his father or uncle. *It was definitely someone he knew,* I thought.

The sound of a siren and flashing lights caught everyone's attention. Daniel's mother had called the police.

"He is four years old," Daniel's mother cried as she talked to the police officer. "Please help me find my son," she pleaded.

"Ma'am, we will do everything we can," the officer assured the mother. "I want everyone to stay calm."

After walking around the block a few times searching for Daniel, my father and his friends returned to the apartment to finish their practice. They had one more song that they needed to rehearse and it was getting dark outside. I sat by the window hoping and praying that Daniel would show up. I began to worry.

I went out to the hallway and looked down the stairway to see if Daniel was there. I didn't see him, but I did see someone standing in front of the door. I could tell by the uniform that the person standing there was a police officer. He was knocking on that stranger's apartment door.

I heard the door open slightly. I could hear the sound of the door chain. It was latched so no one could come in. We had one of those at home. The man peeked through the door and looked at the officer.

"May I help you, sir?" he said.

"Have you seen the little boy from upstairs, Daniel?" the officer asked.

"No, I was sleeping all day," the man said.

What? I thought. *You are lying. I saw you talking to Daniel earlier today.* I wanted to speak out or say something to the officer, but I couldn't. I remembered my mother telling me to always mind my own business. I didn't know what to do.

The officer looked at the man strangely as though he recognized him.

"Well, he is missing and everyone is looking for him. If you happen to have time, please join the search," the officer said.

"Sure, certainly," the man said. "I'll be out soon."

The officer left and the man closed the door. I ran inside to look out the window again. I wanted to yell out to the officer to tell him that the man was lying, but by then the officer had returned to his police car and left.

~

Some time went by when I looked out the window and noticed a huge cloud of blackness coming from down below. Smoke was coming from the window on the first floor. I could feel the heat in the air.

"Fire!" Someone yelled.

I ran to my father. The music was so loud; the men never heard the commotion outside. I tugged at my father's pants.

"Papi, there's a fire. I see smoke!" I said.

The men dropped their instruments and by the time they approached the window, the smoke was intense. Papi grabbed me and carried me in his arms. His friends grabbed their instruments. Papi immediately began to run down the stairs as he led the others.

"Hurry!" He yelled.

When we approached the stairs leading to the first floor, we were stunned by what we saw. There he was, Daniel. He had a towel wrapped around his waist. He looked like he was in shock, almost lifeless. Daniel began to cough. Cheo ran up to him and picked him up. Papi quickly realized that the fire was coming from the first floor. The smoke thickened. We could not escape. We couldn't even see the main entrance.

People were panicking; some were screaming. Everyone felt trapped.

Papi yelled, "Turn around and run to the rooftop!" Everyone fled to the roof. By the time they got there, the fire engines were already outside.

"Keep moving," Papi yelled.

We ran together. Luckily all the apartment buildings on the block were attached and that meant that the rooftops were connected. We jumped from one roof to the next until we reached a building that Papi felt was safe for all of us to enter. Papi opened the door to the roof and we ran down the stairs until we exited the building.

A woman saw Daniel in Cheo's arms.

"Daniel, mi hijo, where have you been? What happened to you?" She screamed as tears flooded her face. She ran up to Cheo and grabbed Daniel.

Papi and Cheo looked at each other. They couldn't believe that they found the missing boy.

"He was standing in the stairway when we found him," Papi said. "Near the fire."

"Where are your clothes? What are you doing with this towel?" She asked. She had so many questions, but was glad to see her little boy alive. She started to cry uncontrollably.

The neighbors gathered around her as she held Daniel. They were happy that she found him. Everyone stood around to watch the firemen. They were working very hard to put out the fire on the first floor.

"It looks like nobody lives in this apartment. There's only a bed and no other furniture," said one of the firemen.

The windows were broken and all kinds of paper were fly-ing out of that first floor apartment. What looked like a piece of paper landed by my feet. I picked it up. It was a picture of a man and a boy. The man was lying in bed next to the boy. They were both naked. I recognized them both. The man was the stranger I had seen earlier talking to Daniel. And the boy… well, he was Daniel. There was so much going on in that moment that I really didn't think about what I had seen in the picture. As soon as I saw Daniel in the picture, I walked over to my father and handed it to him.

"Papi, look," I said.

Papi was busy looking at the burning apartment. When I showed him the picture, he grabbed it and his face turned white as a ghost. Papi grabbed my hand as tightly as he could. He walked over to the police officer who had been out looking for Daniel and gave him the picture.

"My daughter just found this," Papi said to the police officer.

The police officer looked at me and asked me where I got the picture. I told him that it was flying around and landed by feet. I showed him where I found it.

The police officer nodded his head and looked at my father.

"Don't say anything; I will talk to the mother," he said.

The police officer put the picture in his pocket and walked over to Daniel's mother.

"Ma'am, I think you should take Daniel to the hospital," he said. "He should be looked at by a doctor."

Daniel's mother had not seen the picture. She didn't understand what the officer was trying to say, but she agreed to take Daniel to the hospital anyway.

"Okay, sir," she said.

Daniel's mother walked over to a woman who she apparently knew and asked her if she could watch the other three boys.

"Of course, anything for you," the lady said.

She got into the police car with Daniel and the police officer took them to the hospital.

"Papi, why is Daniel going to the hospital?" I asked.

"The doctor needs to make sure that he is all right. That's all," Papi said. He looked like he was worried about something.

My father and I walked through the crowd and passed the burning apartment. No one could possibly be in there now. I overheard one of the firemen say the word *arson*. We started to walk home.

The walk home was pretty long. I guess Papi wanted to take his mind off things so walking was good for him. I didn't mind the walk. I loved walking hand in hand with my father. He held my hand tightly as we walked almost like he was never going to let me go. I was still very curious about the picture.

"Papi, was that Daniel's father sleeping with him?" I asked.

"I don't know hija," Papi said.

Papi didn't like lying to me. He knew the man in the picture was not Daniel's father. I found out later that Daniel's father was in Puerto Rico visiting his sick uncle. Daniel's father's name was Alfonso and he would occasionally come down to Cheo's apartment to hang out with the guys. He also played the guitar.

We made it home in time for Mami's dinner. I couldn't wait to tell her about the fire.

"What fire?" Mami asked as she served dinner.

"There was a lot of smoke and a boy was missing, but then they found him," I said.

"Nina, come sit down. Let's eat dinner," Papi said.

Bobby was already eating. I sat right next to him.

Papi told Mami about the missing boy and the fire in the apartment building. We all sat still and listened as Papi spoke. He left out some things, though. He didn't mention the picture of Daniel and the man, at least not in front of me and Bobby.

"We have to watch our kids every minute," Papi said. "Siempre! You can't trust anyone. Nina, Bobby, don't talk to people you don't know, okay?"

"Okay," Bobby and I said at the same time.

I didn't understand why my father would say that. I wanted to ask Papi what he meant by not trusting anyone, but I got distracted. I began to watch Bobby put food in his mouth. He ate really fast, almost like he was starving.

~

Later that week, I overheard a conversation between Papi and Mami in the kitchen. Papi told Mami that he had run into Daniel's mother, Beatrice. He said that Beatrice told him Daniel was slowly recovering. Beatrice told Papi that Daniel was pretty sedated when my father found him. The fudgesicle that the stranger had given him was laced with some kind of drug. Beatrice thanked my father for finding her son. Papi said that Beatrice began to cry. He said she took a deep breath and hesitated before saying her last words: *Daniel was violated.*

10

The Furry Creature

Time went by and Christmas day was soon approaching. I loved Christmas and everything about it. I loved Santa Claus and presents, but what I loved the most was how all of my cousins and family would come visit me on Christmas Eve. It was two weeks before Christmas when Mami and I began decorating our Christmas tree.

"Mami, why isn't our Christmas tree green?" I asked.

"Because it's aluminum and this one is silver," Mami said.

"Why?" I asked.

"These trees are in style. Remember when you saw it on the Charlie Brown special?" Mami asked.

"Yeah, but I thought it was a different color," I said. "Um, maybe it did look the same." We laughed and talked a lot. I asked my mother what she wanted the most for Christmas.

"Ay, hija, I want peace and quiet," Mami said.

"Mami, you know what I want?" I asked.

"¿Que, hija?" Mami asked.

"You, Papi, me, and Bobby together forever," I said.

Mami smiled. "Me too," she said.

At night, I tossed and turned on my mattress. It started to bother me that I still didn't have a real bed. The lights on the tree were still on; I had asked my parents to leave the tree lights on until I fell asleep. Except for the lights blinking on the tree, the living room was dark. I loved the star on the treetop. The red garland and all of the ornaments made the tree look very nice. I was so proud of how we decorated the tree.

As I lay on my mattress, I began to dream about becoming a doctor. I remember being a patient in the hospital the year prior. I was coughing and spitting really thick spit. My doctor, a tall man with white skin, black hair, and light brown eyes, came in to see me.

"Hi Nina, how are you this morning?" Dr. Abe asked. He had such a beautiful smile.

"Okay," I said as I coughed.

"May I listen to your chest?" he asked.

"Yes," I nodded.

The doctor took a long tubing which split in two at one end and put it in his ears. The other end was a single tube with a sliver round thing at the end. He put the round end on my chest. He made funny faces and made me laugh as he moved the silver thing around on my chest.

"Nina, can you take a deep breath for me?" the doctor asked.

"Yes," I said. I coughed as I tried to fill my chest with fresh air.

"Do you want to listen?" he asked.

"Yes," I said with a smile on my face, eyes wide.

The doctor put the two ends in my ears. Staring at the ceiling with my mouth open, I could hear weird sounds coming from my chest. It almost sounded like my Rice Crispies cereal when I poured milk into it: *snap, crackle, pop.*

"You are getting better, Nina," he said. "You are going home soon."

The doctor and his nurses visited me and my roommates every day. One of the nurses, Cecilia, a plain, dark-haired, blue-eyed, white woman with a thick accent, also came to see me and my roommates. She was the mother of Gina, one of my roommates. Gina was my age and looked like her mother. We would smile at each other whenever we could.

On my last day at the hospital, my doctor came to see me to say goodbye. He even made jokes.

"Knock, knock?" the doctor asked.

"Who's there?" I said.

"Abe!"

"Abe who?"

"Abe C D E F G…!" he said.

I was so impressed by the doctor's funny faces and jokes that right there and then, I knew I wanted to be just like him, a doctor, someone who helps people get better and saves them. I knew that my parents were getting older. Mami was already twenty-five years old and Papi was thirty. I would have to hurry up and become a doctor so that I could take care of them and save their lives one day.

I began to nod off when all of a sudden I heard a noise right next to my mattress. I opened my eyes and saw something moving. I noticed a candy wrapper moving on the floor. When I looked closely, I became terrified of what I saw.

The animal looked like a squirrel. It was tiny and furry with a long skinny tail. I jumped off the mattress.

"Papi!"

I ran to my parent's room.

"There's a little squirrel in the living room," I said. "It was eating candy. Can I sleep with you? I'm scared. I don't want to sleep on that mattress anymore."

"It's probably a mouse, Nina... Okay, come lie down," Papi said.

I jumped on the bed and lay down between my parents.

"Good night," I said.

"Buenas noche," said Mami and Papi.

~

The next morning, I got out of bed quietly. I peeped through my parents' bedroom door to see if the mouse was still there. I saw nothing, not even the candy wrapper. My parents woke up shortly after.

Later that afternoon, Papi and some helpers brought a green sectional sofa into the living room. The helpers took my mattress out to a truck and then brought in a Castro Convertible Ottoman.

"Where's my mattress?" I asked.

"Look Nina, this is your new bed," Mami said. "This thing opens up into a bed. We'll show you."

Papi and Mami unfolded the ottoman and showed me my new twin size bed. I was all smiles. *I won't be sleeping on the floor anymore,* I thought.

"I like my new bed, but what about that mouse? He might come back," I said.

"Don't worry Nina. He won't jump on this bed. He's not coming back," Papi said.

I believed my father. I gave him a hug.

~

Later that evening, I saw Papi put a chunk of cheese on a little wooden board. He pulled back on a metal bar and then placed the board behind the stove.

"What's that Papi?" I asked.

"It's a mouse trap," Papi said. "We are going to catch the mouse you saw last night and take it away from here."

"Thank you, Papi," I said.

I feel asleep that night on my new bed. I went into a deep sleep. Sometime later, I was awakened by a sound coming from the kitchen. I ran into my parents' room.

"Papi, Papi, there's a noise in the kitchen," I said.

Papi got out of bed to check the kitchen. When he finally looked behind the stove, he knew immediately where the noise was coming from. That furry little mouse was caught in the mousetrap.

"Nina, we have him. We got the mouse," Papi said. "Come look."

I got up to look. I took a peek and turned my head. I couldn't stand looking at it.

"Please, please get it out of here. I'm scared," I said.

"It's dead Nina; it's not going to hurt you," Papi said.

"Please, Papi," I pleaded.

My father went back to his bedroom, put on pants over his boxer shorts, and walked back behind the stove. He picked up the mousetrap with his bare hands, opened the door, and carried it outside to the street. Relieved when I saw my father return empty-handed, I took a deep breath and smiled. Papi washed his hands in the bathroom, then kissed me good night.

I smiled and happily went back to sleep.

11

Christmas Eve. 1965.

Nochebuena came around and my mother's anxiety level was sky high. Family and friends were coming that night and there was so much to do. Christmas Eve was a busy day in my house. Mami and Papi were great cooks. Together they made traditional Puerto Rican Christmas foods. Every year Papi helped Mami make the desserts the night before Christmas Eve. Tembleque, a coconut-based pudding, was a popular one in my house and one of my favorites. Coquito, an eggnog made with coconut, eggs, and cinnamon, was another one. When my aunts made their eggnogs, they added a drink called rum, but not my Papi; he didn't like to drink that stuff.

One weekend, Mami and Papi sat in the kitchen all night making pasteles, meat pastries made with pork and wrapped in paper. I wanted to help so I tried to tie the strings around the already-wrapped pasteles.

"Ay, Nina, you have to pull the string ends down this way and turn the pastel over," Mami said as she tried to teach me how to tie the string around the pastel. "Then you bring the string around the ends of the pastel and tie the string in the middle into a knot or bow like this."

"It's hard, Mami. I'm afraid I'm going to squish the pastel," I said.

"It just takes practice," she said.

"Are we going to eat pasteles tonight?" I asked.

"No, I'm going to cook them in a pot with hot water on Christmas Eve," Mami said. "That way we all eat fresh pasteles."

This Christmas Eve fell on a Friday and Papi was off from work early.

"Nina, you and your brother can help clean the house while I cook," Mami said.

"Okay, Mami," I said.

"Manuel, help me here in the kitchen," Mami said.

"Si señora," my father said as he winked at me and gave me a look that said my mother was the boss in the house.

"Papi, is Santa Claus coming tonight?" I asked.

"Si, hija," Papi said.

"You're not getting anything, Nina," Bobby said.

I called out to my father. "Pa—pi, Bobby is mean to me."

"Bobby, be nice," Papi said.

When I walked into the kitchen to get a glass of water, I saw Mami putting a big pork in the oven. *Pernil asado. Mmm, delicious*, I thought. Just the smell of it roasting made me hungry. Later she would be making arroz con gandules, yellow rice with pigeon peas—Puerto Rico's national dish, Papi once told me. I could smell Mami's homemade sofrito, a mix of garlic, peppers, tomatoes, and onions cooked in olive oil. I always liked the smell of sofrito, even though I didn't like the onions; they made me cry whenever I watched Mami cut them.

It didn't take long for Mami and Papi to combine their typical Puerto Rican traditions with the American culture. In New York, Christmas always meant snow, Christmas trees, and Santa Claus. In Puerto Rico, some children received gifts, but not from Santa Claus. Santa couldn't make it to the island with his reindeer in his hot wool suit and hat, or at least that was what Mami told me. The holiday gifts came from Los Reyes.

The Reyes celebrations begin on the eve of the Three King's Day, which is always on the fifth of January. Children place cups of water and grass into shoeboxes and the boxes are placed under their beds for the Three Kings and their camels. The Three Kings come in the middle of the night. The kings drink the water and their camels eat the grass. Los Reyes then fill the shoe boxes with gifts, sweets, and many wonderful things. The Children wake up to find the gifts under their beds.

Parrandas is another tradition that Mami told me about. Puerto Ricans are known for their unforgettable Christmas caroling. Most parranderos, Christmas carolers, play some sort of instrument—guitar, güiro, or palitos. Sometime after 10 p.m., los parranderos walk door-to-door singing Christmas carols as they play their instruments. Traditionally, los parranderos are invited in and refreshments, music, and dance follow. Afterward, they attend the midnight mass at a local church. This is how Puerto Ricans retain their holiday spirit.

My parents kept their Christmas traditions by improvising. They invited their family and friends over to our house every Christmas Eve to eat dinner and listen to my father's band play Christmas music. Then afterward, we would go to mass.

Our family and friends started coming to our house around three in the afternoon. By five p.m., the apartment was full. Mami and her sisters began to serve dinner. The kitchen was small, so a few big people sat in the kitchen to eat while others sat in the living room with their plates on their laps. Most of the kids sat around in a circle on the floor with their plates on their laps.

After dinner, I heard Mami and the women talking in the kitchen as they cleaned up.

"Lydia, the rice is delicious," Tia Josephina, one of Mami's older sisters, said.

"Si, I like el pernil, too!" Tia Blanca, my mother's youngest sister, said.

"Gracias," Mami said. "I think I put too much salt on the pork."

"No, it's good," Millie's mother said.

Meanwhile, the men were in the living room getting their instruments ready. Papi sat on the sofa holding his guitar and moving the strings with his fingers. Felipe sat on the other end of the sofa warming up with his guitar. David stood up as he played el guiro. He held the brown hollow instrument in his left hand and scraped it with what looked like a fork. Cheo played las maracas.

Some of the little kids ran around the apartment playing hide and seek. My cousins from Bay Ridge, Anita and Rosa, sat on the living room floor coloring in their coloring books. Sitting between them, Millie and I could see that Anita and Rosa were very good at coloring. My other cousins from Jersey City, Leticia and Maritza, sat on the floor and played with their dolls. Bobby and Miguel played marbles in Bobby's room.

Once I heard Papi starting to sing, I got up and began clapping my hands.

"Papi, Papi! Sing the El Burrito Sabanero song and... Que Buena es la noche Buena." The kids all jumped up and clapped their hands as they shouted. "Yes, sing Sabanero!" The women came out of the kitchen and began to cheer the men on.

"Manuel, sing," Mami said as she gave Papi a kiss on the cheek.

"Go ahead, Felipe, Cheo, and David," Tia Blanca shouted. "Play the music."

Papi and the guys began to play my favorite Christmas songs. We had such a great time listening and singing along.

Our friends and family left around nine p.m. to return home and to get ready for the midnight Christmas Eve mass at Transfiguration Church. Most of the kids dreaded the one-hour mass. They all just wanted to go home to sleep so that they could wake up in the morning and open their presents. But not me. I liked to pray. Sometimes I asked God for things, just like I did the Christmas Eve before, when I asked for toys.

Other times, I just thanked him for everything. Papi and the priest always said to give thanks to people.

"We have to go to church tonight?" the kids would ask.

"Yes and we don't want to hear any complaints or Santa Claus won't come," the parents would say.

Mass seemed to last a little longer than usual. The church was full; there were people everywhere. Everyone looked nice. The men wore suits and the women wore nice dresses. The kids looked good, too. The church looked beautiful. There were two Christmas trees in front of the altar, lots of garland with lights around the altar, and red flowers on top of the altar. I could smell the candles burning. I could hear a group of people dressed in robes singing as someone played the organ. "Silent Night" and "Let There Be Peace on Earth" were two of my favorite church songs; they were so beautiful. After the last song, people began to walk up to the altar to get bread. It seemed like it took forever for them to get their bread; the lines were long.

By the time mass was over, all the kids were exhausted. My cousins and friends went back to their homes and we went to ours. We went right to bed. Before going to bed, I made sure that the Christmas tree was lit. My parents were in the habit of turning off the tree lights before leaving the house. I made it my responsibility to turn them back on whenever we got home. Christmas Eve was the only time when we left the lights on all night. I also had a habit of looking out the window before I went to bed. I would look up at the sky to see if Santa Claus was coming, but I never did see anything except for stars.

"Please Santa, don't forget me," I begged.

~

On Christmas morning I woke up and found a few presents under the tree.

"Bobby, Mami, Papi! Santa came!" I screamed.

Bobby, Mami, and Papi woke up and sat around the tree with me. Mami walked over to the tree, picked up a present, and handed it to me.

"Here, Nina, this is for you," she said.

I opened my present. It was a box of play dishes.

"This is what I wanted," I said. "Yeah!"

Mami walked over to Bobby and gave him a gift. He ripped the wrapping paper off the box quickly.

"Yeah, yeah! This is what I wanted," he said. It was a Lionel train set.

"Nina, there's one more for you," Papi said.

"What is it? What?" I asked.

Papi walked to the back of the tree and pulled out a box. It was bigger than a shoe box. I wondered what it was.

"Here, Nina," Papi said.

Even though I was eager to see what it was, I took my time opening my gift. I gently removed the wrapping from the box. I wanted to make this moment last. As soon as I uncovered the box and saw what it was, my mouth dropped wide open.

"Chatty Cathy—this is the doll that I always wanted," I said as I hugged the doll.

I quickly took it out of the box and pulled the string on the back of the doll.

"Let's play school," Chatty Cathy said. I pulled the string again.

"I love you," the doll said.

By now, Bobby was angry.

"How come Nina gets two presents and I only get one?" Bobby asked.

"Wait a minute, Bobby," Mami said. "There's another one for you here."

Mami gave him the box and Bobby wasted no time opening it.

"Whoa, Rock'em Sock'em Robots?" Bobby said. "Thank you, Santa Claus! Papi, let's play."

Bobby took out the robots, one red and the other blue. He set them up inside the boxing ring and got the game ready for him and Papi to play. Bobby tried hard to win each round. It was fun to watch them play.

12

Halloween. Brooklyn. 1966.

Halloween was fun for all kids who lived in Brooklyn. Kids loved to wear their costumes and go trick-or-treating. Bobby and I loved it. It was always safe to walk around the streets, going from house to house, store to store asking for treats. People were very generous; they would give out candy pumpkin, Sweet Tarts, lollipops, bubble gum, and money, mostly pennies.

This year I was six years old and old enough to go trick or treating with my brother, just the two of us. The plan was to go trick-or-treating the entire Halloween weekend. To make it even better, Bobby's surprise birthday party was scheduled for Saturday. He was turning ten years old. My parents had been planning his party for a while now. I knew about it and I was very good at keeping secrets.

"Don't tell Bobby," Mami said.

"I won't," I promised.

It was Friday afternoon. Mami left work early and picked me up from Carmen's house. I was waiting for Bobby to get home from school. I had my costume already laid out on the sofa. Peanuts' Lucy Halloween costume was my favorite. I loved the vinyl blue dress and face mask. I remembered watching Charlie Brown's *It's the Great Pumpkin* on television the night before. Although Lucy came across as a mean person, especially toward her brother Linus, I could see the goodness in her. I was impressed by what Lucy did when she woke up in the middle of the night and saw that Linus was not in his bed. Lucy found her brother asleep in the pumpkin patch, brought him home, took his shoes off, and put him to bed. Lucy really cared about her brother, just like I cared about my brother Bobby.

"Bobby, I can't wait to wear my Lucy costume and go trick-or-treating tonight," I said.

"My costume is not as nice as yours, but that's okay," Bobby said, trying to be nice to me for once. "Just be good when we go out."

"But Bobby, I like how you paint your face and dress up every year. You look kind of scary to me," I said.

"Yeah, but all I wear is a pair of worn baggy jeans and an old shirt. You have a nice costume that Papi bought you," Bobby said.

"Maybe with the money we get from trick-or-treating, we'll be able to buy you a costume," I said.

"Nah, I really don't want to buy one; I like making my own," Bobby said.

We went out trick-or-treating. We stopped at all the stores and apartment buildings on Hooper Street.

"And who are you supposed to be?" asked a lady at her door.

"Lucy, from Charlie Brown," I said.

"And you?" she asked Bobby.

"I'm a bum," Bobby said.

"Well, here's some candy," the lady said.

"Thank you!" we both said.

We walked to Broadway Avenue. I saw skeletons, witches, and fairies walking everywhere. There were so many kids and they all looked nice in their costumes. We were all laughing and having a good time. Before we knew it, our pumpkins were filled to the top with candy and coins. When we got home, Bobby and I counted all the coins; we had exactly ten dollars.

~

The next day was a special day. It was Saturday, Bobby's birthday.

"Bobby, take Nina with you today and be home by five p.m.," Mami said.

"Five o'clock? Mami, it's already two o'clock," Bobby said.

"Just be home by five to eat dinner and you can go back out afterward. Your cousins are coming over tonight," Mami said as she winked at me.

I tried to wink back. I wanted to smile but managed to control myself. I didn't want to give away our secret; today was Bobby's surprise birthday party. This morning, I overheard

Mami telling Papi that the guests would be here by 4:30 p.m. Mami had all the decorations and gifts hidden under her bed. Papi was in charge of bringing home the cake.

"Nina, get your costume on, we're leaving now," Bobby said.

I ran to the living room, picked up my costume, and within seconds, I had it on.

"Mami, can you tie this?" I asked.

Mami walked over and tied the string on the back of my vinyl dress.

Bobby painted his face, put on his old flannel shirt and changed into his worn jeans. Within minutes, we were out the door.

We left the house by 2:30 p.m. Mami looked out the window and watched us as we walked to the street corner. We crossed South 2nd Street and continued on to Hooper Street.

"Bobby, let's go here," I said, bouncing from foot to foot toward a grocery store.

"Okay Nina, but wait for me. You have to stay close to me," he said.

Our pumpkins were filling up fast. I started to feel the weight in my hands.

"My pumpkin feels heavy, Bobby," I said.

"Do you want me to carry it for you?" he asked.

"No, I can carry it."

"Let's turn around now. Its four o'clock and we have to make it home by five," Bobby said.

"Okay," I said.

We walked back up an entire block on Broadway Avenue and when we got to the corner we crossed the street to get to the other side of Hooper Street. We continued trick-or-treating as we walked back home and our pumpkins grew heavier and heavier. We stopped at a bodega in the middle of the block of Hooper Street between South 3rd and South 2nd Streets and right before we walked in, I noticed a tall, dark-skinned man with an afro standing in front of the store. I had never seen him before. *He is not from the neighborhood*, I thought.

Bobby and I got our treat from the owner of the store; he gave us a lot of candy. We left the store and continued to walk home. By this time, I was holding my pumpkin with both hands, practically hugging it. Bobby carried his pumpkin by the handle and held it in his right hand.

Before I knew it, the dark-skinned man who was standing in front of the bodega came running toward us. The man ran into Bobby, pushed him to the ground, and grabbed Bobby's pumpkin. Bobby was shocked. He couldn't believe what had happened.

I screamed, "No, that's my brother's!"

The man didn't even look back. He kept running, turned the corner on South 3rd Street, and disappeared. I was screaming. Tears began pouring down my face.

"Bobby! Bobby! Are you okay?" I asked, my face draining of color.

"Nina, I'm okay! Don't worry," he said as he got up. "I'm

not hurt."

I dropped my pumpkin and quickly hugged my brother. I kept crying and crying.

By this time, there were people everywhere. They must have heard my scream.

"Are you okay?" asked a passerby.

"Yeah, I'm okay," replied Bobby. "Let's go home, Nina."

Bobby helped me pick up my pumpkin and decided to carry it for me. This time he was using both hands to hold it. I could not stop crying. I was so devastated. *How could someone do that?* I thought. *It's his birthday today.*

Upon arriving at our apartment building, I ran up the stoop and up the stairs toward my apartment. Bobby followed.

"Mami! Papi!" I cried as I ran through the door. The apartment was filled with cousins, aunts and uncles.

Mami took a look at me and panicked. "¿Que paso?" she asked.

"Ma—mi, somebody took Bobby's pumpkin!" I said, sniffling as I choked back tears, my voice quivering.

Bobby walked through the door. Mami seemed relieved to see him. By the looks of me, she must have thought that Bobby was terribly hurt.

"Bobby! ¿Estás bien?" Mami asked. She grabbed Bobby and gave him a big hug.

"Si, Mami," he said. "Some man pushed me to the ground and stole my pumpkin."

"Did anyone call the police?" Mami asked.

"No," Bobby responded as he was looking around the room taking note of the decorations. He realized then that Mami and Papi had planned a surprise birthday party for him. He smiled as he looked at his cousins, Junior, Anita, Rosa, Leticia, and Maritza.

"Then I will," Mami said.

~

The police arrived and filed a report. Bobby and I told the police officer what the thief looked like. We also told the officers which way the thief ran. The officer promised us that they would catch the man. Soon after the police left, Papi showed up with a big white box.

"What's going on?" Papi asked.

Mami told him what had happened to Bobby.

"Thank God they're okay," Mami said.

Papi put the box on the table and hugged Bobby.

"Are you okay?" he asked.

"Yes, Papi, I'm okay," Bobby said.

"But the man stole Bobby's pumpkin," I said. My eyes filled with tears again.

"Nina, don't worry about it," Bobby said. "We can go trick-or-treating again tomorrow."

I hugged Bobby tightly and dried my eyes on his shirt. I stepped back. *Wait, I have an idea,* I thought. I ran to the kitchen to get my pumpkin.

"Here Bobby, I have a present for you. You can keep this!" I said as I handed over my pumpkin.

"No, Nina. That's yours," Bobby said.

"It's your birthday; keep it," I said. "It's a birthday present from me."

Bobby didn't want to argue with me. The pumpkin was filled with coins and candy, so he took the pumpkin and hid it in his room. By the time he came out of his room, Mami had already lit the candles on his birthday cake.

"Let's sing happy birthday to Bobby," Mami said.

Bobby sat at the middle of the table in front of the cake. I stood by him. My cousins gathered around the table. Mami began taking pictures of Bobby and all the kids. Papi grabbed his guitar and began to sing "Happy Birthday" in English. Everybody sang along. Then we sang the song in Spanish, "Cumpleaños Feliz." Smiling and eyes twinkling, Bobby made a wish, took a deep breath, and blew out the candles.

After Mami cut and served the cake, Bobby sat on a chair and opened his gifts. By the end of the night, he had completely forgotten about the thief who had stolen his pumpkin... and so had I.

13

A Cold Night. 1967.

January came around and snow fell once again. Our apartment was just as cold inside as it was outside.

"Ay Dios mío, que frio," Mami said.

She picked up el cucharón and walked over to the radiator. She banged and banged on the radiator, hoping to get more heat. The clattering sound was loud enough to wake everyone in the building, but after a few minutes we could actually see more steam coming out. It worked every time.

By now we were used to wearing layers of clothing to bed. I didn't mind sleeping in my polka dot flannel pajamas and sweater.

"Let's drink some hot chocolate," Mami said.

Bobby and I walked to the kitchen and pulled out a chair. We sat at the table and waited for Mami to pour us our hot chocolate.

"Mami, my cho-co-LA-tay is too hot," I said.

"Oh, Nina, stop being a baby. It's not hot," Bobby said.

"I'm not a baby. Stop calling me that," I said. "I'm going to be seven in a couple of days."

"Okay, ya! Sin peleas, por favor," Mami yelled. "No fighting, please."

As soon as we saw Mami's narrowing eyes and serious look on her face, we shut up right away. We knew she was getting angry. There was something else going on with Mami. She seemed like she had been worrying about something all evening. She walked over to the refrigerator and grabbed the glass-bottled milk that the milkman had delivered this morning. She poured some milk in my hot chocolate without even thinking about it. Next thing we knew, my hot chocolate was spilling on the table.

"Caramba!" she yelled. She grabbed the dishcloth and began to clean up the mess.

"It's okay, Mami. Gracias, Mami," I said. I looked at Bobby and gave him a look. *Say something,* I thought.

"Yes, thank you Mami," he said.

We wanted to see her smile. She hadn't been doing much of that lately. Mami looked lonely and sad the last couple of days. Papi hadn't been around very much. He would come home from work, eat, take a bath, and leave with his guitar. He was at band practice all the time. I heard him talking to Mami last week about an upcoming gig.

"Our band is playing next Saturday at a big club," Papi said to Mami.

"What club?" Mami asked. "I am tired of you always being out with the guys."

"It's money" Papi said. "Money for us. The club manager

hired my band to play and it's our first time playing there."

Mami shook her head. I could see the sadness in her eyes. Mami walked away from Papi and went right into her bedroom. Papi lowered his head. He too looked sad.

Mami looked like she was in another world tonight. She didn't talk much and she kept pacing back and forth to her bedroom window. She would look out the window as though she was looking for someone. She kept glancing at the clock. Normally we would sit around the table and talk about anything and everything, but not tonight. Bobby and I could tell she wasn't in the mood to talk.

We drank our hot chocolate and went to bed. Mami tucked us in and made sure that we were completely covered by our blankets. She kissed us on our foreheads and said good night.

"Buenas noche," she said.

"Buenas noche," Bobby and I said at the same time.

Mami walked over to her room and closed the door. From where I was lying in the living room, I could hear a faint sound coming from her room. I jumped out of my Castro Convertible bed and tiptoed to her door. I could now hear clearly what the sound was. Mami was crying.

I wanted to go in her room so bad. I wondered why she was sad. Deep down inside, I knew that she was crying for my father. My mother missed him very much. I missed him too! My father was a hard worker. He worked his full-time job and played in the band. By this time, he was making a lot of money. He even bought a car—a beautiful 1957 Chevy. It was silver with leather interior. I loved riding in the front seat.

I nodded off and must have gone into a deep sleep because when I woke up, it was to the sound of Mami and Papi arguing. Papi had just come home from band practice. He must have sneaked in because I didn't even hear the door open. It was dark inside the apartment. The light from my parents' bedroom was the only light on in the entire apartment. I looked at the window in the living room and noticed that it was also dark outside. I turned to the cuckoo clock on the wall and saw that it was 2 o'clock in the morning.

"I am tired of you coming home late. Estoy cansada," Mami yelled.

"But I am making money. What do you want from me?" Papi asked.

"I don't believe that!" she said. "You just want to be with your friends!"

"I can't believe you!" Papi yelled back. "I'm tired and I'm going to bed."

"No, you are not. You need to get out of here. I'm throwing you out!" Mami said.

"What? I'm not going anywhere," Papi said.

"Go! Leave right now!" Mami yelled with tears in her eyes. She began to walk toward Papi.

Papi backed up, looked at Mami, and took his keys.

"Okay, me voy!" Papi said. He grabbed his coat and walked out the door. I heard the sound of the door slamming. Mami ran to her bedroom and closed the door behind her. I could hear her crying all over again.

I pretended that I was sleeping the whole time my parents were arguing. I had covered my head with my pillow. I couldn't believe my mother threw my father out. I felt my heart pounding as tears began to fill my eyes. My father was the love of my life. The thought of losing him was too much for me. I wanted to scream, but instead I cried silently, *Pa-pi, Pa-pi,* until I fell asleep.

~

I woke up hoping that I'd had a bad dream. My eyes were so swollen from crying during the night that I could hardly open them. I peeked into my parents' bedroom to see if Papi was there, but he wasn't. I realized that my nightmare was actually true, and I faced the heart-wrenching reality of my father leaving us.

It was tough getting ready for school knowing that my Papi had left. I was so angry at Mami for kicking him out. I knew that Mami was also angry so I didn't dare say anything to her. I just got dressed and walked to school alone. I didn't feel like talking to anyone. Bobby had left for school before me so I didn't know if he was upset or not.

Snow was coming down and it was freezing outside. I was bundled up to the point where I looked like an Eskimo. I pushed myself and walked as fast as I could. The cold wind blew against my face, making my tears feel like icicles. Even with my mittens on, my fingers were freezing. I kept rubbing my hands together, trying to keep my fingers warm.

Although the school was only two-and-a-half blocks away from home, the freezing cold made it seem like I had walked miles to school. I felt relief when I got there. I ran up the steps and through the steel doors. I couldn't wait to find some heat. I took off my coat and hung it on the rack that was mounted on the wall in the hallway near my homeroom.

I sat by the window in my homeroom class. The radiator next to me was nice and warm. I could feel my fingers thawing. As I looked through the window, I could see the snow getting heavier by the minute. Parked cars were covered in snow. The streets were icy and cars were sliding everywhere. Hoping to see my father, I kept looking at the cars as they passed by the school.

Papi, where are you? I wondered. *Are you staying warm?*

I imagined my father sleeping in his car, struggling to stay warm. I felt my heart racing as my eyes started to well up again. I put my head down and covered my face so that no one would see me cry.

"Nina Tavarez," Mrs. Stein said as she took attendance.

I raised my hand. "Here," I said without looking and kept my head down.

Mrs. Stein knew that something was bothering me from the moment I walked into the classroom. A great teacher, Mrs. Stein was kind and, most importantly, she understood us. There were so many kids around her desk when I walked in. I was hoping that she didn't notice my swollen eyes when I walked passed her. After she finished taking attendance, Mrs. Stein approached me. For a moment there was silence in the classroom. I didn't realize that everyone was looking at me.

"Nina, are you all right?" she asked.

I covered my face and shook my head. As I drew my next breath, I totally lost it and began to cry uncontrollably. "I don't feel good," I managed to say.

"Come with me, Nina. Let's go to the nurse," Mrs. Stein said. She put her arms around me and tried to comfort me as she wiped my tears away.

We walked over to the school nurse. Mrs. Stein whispered something in her ear. The nurse asked me to lie down and took my temperature. She looked at the glass thermometer and nodded.

"Are you having pain anywhere?" She asked. I shook my head no.

"You have a fever; I need to call home and ask someone to come get you," she said.

I nodded and said, "Okay." I didn't feel like being in school anyway.

~

Mami arrived in a taxi about half an hour later. The taxi driver waited for us in his cab. The nurse told her about my fever.

"Her temperature is 102 degrees," the nurse said. "You

should take her to the doctor."

"Okay," Mami said.

"Something else you should know," the nurse added.

"Yes?" Mami said with a curious look on her face.

"Nina has been crying all morning. Is there something going on at home?" she asked.

Mami's face turned red and tears welled in her eyes. She nodded.

"My husband and I had a fight last night... maybe she is worried," Mami said. "I'll take her to the doctor now."

I kept my head down as I listened to Mami speak. I couldn't even look at her. I was so mad at her. Mami put her arms around me and gave me a hug.

"Here Nina, put on your coat. Let's go see Dr. Cohn. We'll take care of you," Mami said. "Everything will be all right."

As soon as the taxi driver saw us come out, he stepped out of the taxi and opened the rear passenger door for me to sit. Mami sat in the back right next to me.

"Take us to Dr. Cohn's office on South 2nd and Hooper Street," Mami said.

"Yes, Ma'am," he said.

Dr. Cohn's office was right around the corner from where we lived. Whenever my friends and I walked by, we would see the sign on his window that read *Dr. Cohn's Office*. The blinds on the windows were always down so we were never able to look inside. My parents always liked Dr. Cohn. He took care of us right away whenever we went there. The doctor was

American and only spoke English. He was a tall man with a big belly, gray hair, and wrinkles on his face that reminded me of a grandfather.

"Hi, Nina, how are you?" he asked. "Your mother said you are not feeling well. What's wrong?"

"I don't feel good," I said.

"Let me take your temperature," he said. I opened my mouth and once again a glass thermometer went in my mouth. I hated thermometers. It was hard for me to keep my mouth closed while having that thing in there. After a few minutes, the doctor took out the thermometer and read the temperature.

"104 degrees; you are burning up," he said.

Mami raised her eyebrows. Her eyes were darting everywhere. I could see the worried look on her face. She seemed helpless.

"What are you going to do for her?" Mami asked.

"Well for now, I'm going to give her medicine for the fever," he said.

He opened his medicine cabinet and gave me two pink pills. I held them in my hands. *Little pills,* I thought. He gave me a cup of water and I swallowed each pill, one at a time. I drank all the water. I was so thirsty. I could feel my body heating up.

"Okay, now let's get you in the bathtub. I'm going to fill it with ice to try to bring your fever down," he said.

He walked over to the bathtub in his bathroom to make sure that it was clean. Mami trusted the doctor so she did whatever he said.

"Ready, Nina?" Mami asked.

I nodded and said, "Yes."

Mami undressed me down to my panties. She carried me into the bathtub. I sat there with my knees to my chest, trying to cover my bare chest. Mami sat in a chair next to the tub and watched Dr. Cohn fill the bathtub with ice. He kept dumping buckets and buckets of ice into the tub. Once the ice covered me from the waist down, Dr. Cohn stopped bringing ice.

"I'm going to leave you in the bathtub for a few minutes, Nina," he said. He looked at Mami and added, "Please watch her for me while I see the other patient in the waiting room."

"Okay," Mami said.

She put her hand on my shoulder. "Nina, are you all right?"

"A-hum," I managed to say.

My body began to shiver and every muscle began to twitch. I could see myself in the mirror on the wall. I started clenching my teeth. My color left me and I became white as a ghost. Next thing I knew, I fell into a deep sleep.

~

"Dr. Cohn, Dr. Cohn!" Mami screamed.

The doctor came running in and saw me lying in the ice asleep. He grabbed a blanket and covered me as he lifted me out of the bathtub. He held me close to try to keep me warm.

"What is happening to my daughter?" Mami screamed.

"Tell me!"

By now, Mami was crying hysterically.

"She's having a seizure," he said. "She'll come out of it."

"Ay Dios mío! Help her please," she pleaded with God.

Several minutes went by and I woke up, but I was still very sleepy.

"Mami," I said.

"Mi hija!" she said as she hugged me. I tried to hug her back.

"She'll be all right now," Dr. Cohn said. "Let's get her dressed. She can go home. I'm going to give you some medicine to give her at home," he said.

"She's okay?" Mami asked.

"Yes, she will be okay," he said.

Mami got me dressed as fast as she could. Dr. Cohn volunteered to carry me home. He carried me into the apartment and laid me down on my Castro Convertible bed that was still opened. I had been too angry this morning to put it away like I normally did. Mami quickly covered me with a blanket. I could hear Dr. Cohn give my mother instructions before he left. I fell asleep as soon as I heard the door close.

I kept dozing on and off for the rest of the day. At times, I could hear my mother talking on the phone with some of my aunts. She told them what had happened. I could hear her crying. I also heard her talk about the fight that she had with my father.

"Si, we had a fight last night. I told Manuel to leave," I

heard Mami say. "I don't know what to do. I still love him and Nina loves him very much. That's her father!"

Later in the evening, I heard a knock on the door. I was still in bed, but I could see Mami looking through the peephole. She put the chain on the door.

"Let me in," I heard someone yelling. The voice sounded like my father's.

"No, I'm not going to let you in," Mami said.

"I want to see my daughter!" Papi said.

He unlocked the door with his key but was unable to get in. That dumb chain was in the way.

"Let me in! I heard she is sick," he yelled.

"No!" Mami said and started to cry.

"Please, Lydia. Let me in," Papi said.

I sat up in bed at the sound of his voice. I wanted to get up and run to him, but my legs were too weak. I started to cry.

"Papi, Papi!' I screamed. I took a deep breath, "Mami, please, please let him in!"

Mami saw the tears in my eyes. She paused for a moment before taking the chain off the door to let my father in. Papi ran to me and hugged me. I felt a sense of relief, but I couldn't stop crying. "Papi, I missed you!" I said. I hugged him so hard; I didn't want to let him go.

"Nina, I missed you too!" he said. "You are sick?"

"Yes, Papi. I couldn't stop thinking about you in school today. It made me sick just thinking that I would never see you again. Don't ever leave me," I said.

"I never wanted to leave you," he said as he hugged me. I could see the tears in his eyes.

Mami watched us with her swollen eyes. She looked like she was ready to cry again as she sat on the sofa. She walked over to us and gave us both a big hug.

"I'm so sorry, Nina. Perdóname Manuel," she said.

Papi hugged her back. I could hear Mami crying on Papi's shoulder.

"I feel bad. I should have never asked you to leave," Mami cried.

"Ya, ya no llores," Papi said. Papi held her face in his hands and wiped away her tears. Mami looked into his eyes, and suddenly, they started kissing. It was so nice to see them together. Watching Papi and Mami kiss was so beautiful.

Papi and Mami tucked me in and kissed me good night. After that, they both went to their bedroom and I didn't see them for the rest of the night. As I lay in bed, I made the sign of the cross and said a prayer. I thanked God for keeping my family together. I couldn't stop smiling... I was so happy.

14

Gina. 1968.

By the fall of 1968, I was eight years old and had already become popular in my neighborhood with both girls and boys. A champ at playing stickball and Skelsy, I was also good at jumping Double Dutch. Fast on my feet, I was able to enter the ropes from any angle.

One of the girls with whom I played Double Dutch, Gina Talarico, became one of my closest friends. She and I met in the hospital when we were both sick. Her mother, Cecilia, was a nurse there. Gina and I would jump rope every chance we could during recess in the schoolyard of P.S. 19. We became close friends in second grade and by third grade, Gina became one of my best friends. We would always kid around about how similar our names sounded.

"Gina and Nina. We sound like twins," Gina once said as we sat next to each other in the schoolyard.

"Yeah, that's true. Maybe we could be sisters," I said. "I don't have any."

"Well, I have two sisters and a brother, but you can still be my sister," Gina said.

"I speak Spanish; do you?" I asked Gina.

"No, I speak Italian, but I think it all sounds alike," Gina said.

We were always together in school during recess. Gina was my height and weight, with dark hair and blue eyes. She looked like her mother, as did her sisters and brother. Gina and I didn't see each other after school or on weekends very much because Gina lived in a different section of Williamsburg. I lived too far away to walk to her house.

Gina's brother, Anthony, was fourteen years old. Anthony was tall and skinny. Her older sister, Mary, was fifteen and her younger sister, Theresa, was six years old. I met all of them one day when I was shopping with Mami on Broadway Avenue. They were with their mother. Gina loved her siblings and her mother, Cecilia. She always bragged about her mother being a nurse. Gina never really talked about her father. At times, she said that he was not a nice man. I never asked why.

~

One day, after playing Double Dutch in the schoolyard, I glanced over at Gina and told her that I was glad that we were friends. Gina hugged me and said that she was happy too. We were dismissed at three p.m. from school that day. Gina's mother and little sister were outside in a black car waiting for Gina to come out. Gina waved goodbye to me as she jumped in the car. I waved back and began to walk home with friends from my neighborhood.

Getting homework done as soon as they got home from school was routine for Gina and her siblings; their mother demanded that of them. She wanted to make sure that her kids got their homework done before she left for work at the hospital to begin her second shift. Gina's father worked long hours. He had some kind of office job.

The kids watched each other whenever their parents weren't around. When their parents were gone, the kids would play around the house in every room, except for one. They were not allowed in their father's office, and because they all feared their father, they usually obeyed the rule—except on this one fateful day.

About an hour after Gina's mother left for work, Anthony decided to go outside to play with his skateboard. Mary sneaked out to see her boyfriend and she put Gina in charge of Theresa.

"Watch her," Mary said to Gina. "And don't go near Father's office!"

"Okay," Gina said.

As soon as Mary left, Gina and Theresa looked at each other. They were up to something all right. They were going to do it; they were going to go into the forbidden room.

They looked through everything in the office, the filing cabinets, and the desk drawers. When they opened one of the desk drawers, they were stunned by what they saw.

It was a black gun.

Gina and Theresa were so afraid of it that they didn't dare touch it.

"Is Father a police officer?" Theresa asked.

"I don't know," Gina responded.

As they looked through the filing cabinets, they came across a file containing news articles. Gina read one of the articles, which was about a mobster in New York City who had committed homicide. Apparently, he had killed a lot of people that same year.

"Maybe Father's a lawyer," Gina said.

Theresa kept jumping around, looking through everything. She even opened the closet door.

"More filing cabinets," Theresa said.

Gina stopped reading the articles and walked over to the closet. She thought the filing cabinets inside the closet were tall. The girls came to a sudden halt when they looked up at the ceiling and noticed a big hole, more like a secret passageway with some light up there. They became even more curious.

"I want to look up there," Theresa said. "Hold me up."

At first, Gina said no, but she changed her mind and then agreed. They pulled a chair to the closet and climbed on the filing cabinets. Gina held Theresa up until she made it to the hole. Theresa pulled herself up and soon she was in what appeared to be a secret room.

Theresa looked around. Within a matter of seconds, she stumbled upon a blonde little girl who was tied up. Trembling in fear, Theresa screamed in her breaking voice at the sight of the little girl lying face down. The girl looked like she was sleeping. Her mouth was covered with a huge piece of silver tape. She was wearing a hospital gown, the kind that Theresa's mother used to bring home from the hospital for the kids to wear at home before going to bed.

"Theresa, what do you see?" Gina yelled.

"Oh, no!" She's not moving!" Theresa cried.

"Who?" Gina asked.

Gina froze when she turned around and saw a man standing right behind her.

"What are you girls doing up there? You're not supposed to be in here!" he yelled.

It was Gina's father and he was very angry. He quickly grabbed Gina by the arm and threw her across the room. Gina banged her head against one of the filing cabinets. She lost consciousness and blood began pouring from the back of her head.

Gina's father was furious. Blinded by his anger, he lost total control of himself. He was now another person. He climbed on top of the filing cabinet and went after Theresa.

"Come here!" he yelled.

Theresa was terrified. She cried and screamed for help. She tried to get away, but there were no exits. Her father made it to the top. He grabbed Theresa and covered her mouth to keep her from screaming. Within seconds, the screaming stopped.

Gina's father came back down. He saw Gina lying on the floor. He noticed the blood and that she was not breathing. He held his hands to his face and began to cry.

"Oh my God, what did I do?" he cried. "I can't believe that I killed my two precious little daughters."

Gina's father paced back and forth around the room as he cried out loud. He pulled at his hair and began banging his head on the wall. He walked over to his desk as desperation began to sink in. He took a deep breath and tried to take control of himself. He picked up a pen and paper and wrote a long note as fast as he could. He then reached into his drawer and pulled out his gun. It was the black gun that the girls had found earlier. Gina's father took the gun and held it to his head. He closed his eyes and took a deep breath as he pulled the trigger.

15

The Next Day

I walked to school with my friends Sara, Blanca, and Millie. We shared jokes and laughed about anything. We got along very well. We made it to homeroom on time. *Phew!* I was worried about getting in late. The bell rang as soon as I walked in. The girls made it to their homerooms as well. As the teacher took roll call, I looked around the classroom for my friend Gina and noticed that her seat was empty. *Maybe she's sick*, I thought.

Around 10:30 a.m., right before recess, the principal stopped by the classroom to speak with my teacher. It wasn't very often that I would see the principal here in my class. After their brief conversation, I noticed my teacher's reaction. She looked like she was ready to cry; her face had lost its color. It was bad news all right, but I didn't know what had happened.

The principal asked for our attention. All of the students turned around and gave him their undivided attention. We knew that something was wrong.

"I have bad news for you," the principal said. He hesitated before he spoke again. "One of your classmates passed away last night. Gina Talarico was taken to the hospital last night and died."

"What?" the students screamed. They were shocked. I covered my face and broke down into tears.

"No, you are wrong. She can't be dead!" I screamed and cried uncontrollably. I could feel my heart pounding. "No, that's not true! That's a lie; she's alive!"

My teacher came to me and gave me a big hug. She tried to console me, but I simply lost it. I was crying my eyes out. My best friend was dead. It was so unreal. Within seconds, I could hear my classmates crying.

"Come on Nina, let's go to the nurse," my teacher said.

The teacher walked me to the nurse's office. However, not even the nurse could make it better. She called home to speak with one of my parents and luckily she was able to reach my father.

"I'll be right there," Papi said.

By the time Papi arrived at the nurse's office, I was in a deep sleep, and no matter how hard he tried to wake me, he couldn't. He carried me to his car and drove me home. I woke up as he tried to lift me out of the car. I began to cry hysterically again. We got to the apartment and he laid me down on the sofa.

Papi held me close and looked as though he was about to cry, too. I could tell that he was feeling my pain.

"I know, Nina," Papi said. He got me a pillow and covered me with a blanket.

"Nina, do you want to eat?" he asked.

"No, Papi, I'm not hungry," I said. "I just want to sleep."

Papi stared at me as I tried to sleep. I could see tears in his eyes now. I dozed off into a deep sleep. Mami got home from work a little past four p.m. She had gone to Carmen's house to get me, but Carmen told her that I was upstairs with my father.

"¿Que paso?" she asked Papi.

"Shh!" he said

Papi escorted Mami into the kitchen and told her what had happened. He explained that he had come home from work early because he had not been feeling well. He said that as soon as he walked in, the school nurse called.

"But what happened to Gina," Mami asked.

Papi looked at Mami and said, "I'll show you." He left the apartment to go to his car to get the newspaper. He read the front page to Mami as he translated the article from English to Spanish.

"Apparently, Frank Talarico killed his daughter Gina and then tried to kill Theresa. Miraculously, Theresa lost consciousness when he covered her mouth and managed to survive. Mr. Talarico then committed suicide. The newspaper implied that Frank Talarico was involved with the mob. He had kidnapped a little girl and held her hostage in the attic to get revenge on her father who had wronged him. A medical examiner revealed that the little girl in the attic had died from dehydration and heat exhaustion. Gina died from a head injury and a broken neck," Papi said.

Mami began to cry. "Oh my God, I can't believe it."

I slept all through the night and even missed school the next day. Carmen stayed home with me while my parents were at work.

~

As weeks went by, we learned more about Gina's death. Theresa had provided more detailed information to the police. I still could not get over Gina's death. There were days when I felt mute and like I had lost my will to live. I was just going through the motions. But my deep sorrow gradually went away over the next few months. Writing and drawing pictures seemed to help my pain a little. I began to draw pictures of Gina and me in my notebook jumping Double Dutch. On one page I drew a picture of Gina with a cross above her head and angels by her side. What really helped me the most was the support that I received from my parents and church; they became my saviors.

Papi and Mami once told me that whenever I felt pain in my heart, I should pray hard for God to take it all away. Papi even gave me a rosary to keep under my pillow at night.

"God will make it better, Nina," Papi would say.

"Gina is in a good place," Mami would also say.

So I prayed for Gina every time we went to church and before going to bed at night. I also prayed for Gina's mother, her sisters Mary and Theresa, and brother Anthony, even though I never saw them again.

"God, please take good care of them. And Gina, I will never forget you."

16

Stranger by the School
Yard. 1969.

April 30, 1969 was a nice, cool day. The sun was shining brightly without a cloud in the sky. Six months after Gina's death, I was starting to feel more at peace and like myself again. My classmates and I were playing dodgeball in the schoolyard during recess. We normally played dodgeball in the gymnasium, but today we played outside. The main objective of the game was to eliminate all members of the opposing team by hitting them with thrown balls. We all avoided being hit with the balls. My team was good. We were able to catch the thrown balls and eliminate the players who threw the balls at us. The game was always intense. There were balls flying everywhere.

"Watch out!" I yelled to Sara.

"I got this!" Sara said.

"I'll get that one," I said.

I ran to the chain-link fence where the ball had landed. It was near the entrance to the school. As I approached the fence, I noticed a man with dark hair standing on the opposite side of the fence. He was staring at me as he looked through the fence. I didn't recognize him. I could tell he wasn't from the neighborhood. When you lived in my area, you kind of got to know who your neighbors were. He was one of those who didn't belong. I noticed his sliver car parked close to him. He had left the front passenger door wide open. As I approached the ball the man spoke to me.

"Hi," he said.

I looked at him but didn't say a word. The man gave me the creeps. *Thank goodness he's behind the fence,* I thought. I walked up to the ball cautiously, grabbed it, and began to walk away.

"Do you want some money?" he asked. I stopped and turned around. I looked at him and acted like I was listening.

"I'll give you a dollar if you get in the car with me," he said.

In shock, I shook my head and began to run away. "No way," I shouted.

I ran to the gym teacher as fast as I could. Luckily, my teacher, Mrs. Smith, was talking to the principal.

"Mrs. Smith, Mrs. Smith, that man asked me to get in the car with him!" I said.

"What man?" Mrs. Smith asked.

"That one over there!" I said as I pointed toward the man.

Mrs. Smith and the principal turned around and saw the stranger getting into his car. He started the car and took off.

"Nina, what did he look like?" Mrs. Smith asked.

"He was tall and had dark hair. Oh yeah, he was American, too!" I said.

The principal began sidestepping, but kept his eyes on the stranger's car. He tried to read the license plate, but the car was too far away. He asked all the students to come back inside.

"Come on, let's get in the gym, now!" he said.

After all the students were in the gym, the principal went to his office and called the police. I was called to the office after the police arrived. The officer began to ask me questions.

"What did he look like?" he asked.

I repeated what I had told Mrs. Smith. "He was tall, had dark hair, white skin, and was American," I said.

"How do you know he was American?" the police officer asked.

"The way he talked English," I said.

"Okay, what did he say to you?" the officer asked.

I stuck to my story. I repeated everything the man said to me. I even described the silver car he was driving. The principal jumped in and confirmed what I was saying.

"Yes, I saw him too. He got in his silver car and drove away," the principal said.

"Okay, I'm going to take this information down to the station. If you see him again, call the police. And Nina, don't ever go near him," the police officer said.

"Okay, sir," I said.

The police officer left. By this time, the dismissal bell rang and all the kids were dismissed.

I walked home with my friends Miguel, Sara, Millie, and Blanca. We stayed close as we talked about the incident at school.

"Boy, that was creepy," I said.

"I wonder what he wanted," Sara said.

"Where was he going to take you?" Miguel asked.

"I don't know," I said. "The officer said that if I see him again, I should stay away and call the police."

"It sounds scary," Blanca said. "But I would have taken the money and ran." She tried to act tough all the time, like she wasn't afraid of anything.

"No you wouldn't!" Sara, Miguel, and I said at the same time.

"Uh-huh!" Blanca said.

"Yeah, we need to go home and tell our parents," I said.

~

That evening, my parents and I sat down for dinner. I looked up at them and told them about the stranger, including what he looked like and I how I reported everything to the teacher and principal.

"Ay, Dios mio! What did the principal do?" Mami asked.

"He called the police and an officer came to the school. The officer asked me questions and I told him what I saw. The police are out looking for the man," I said.

"Nina, por favor, stay away from strangers. There are a lot of bad people out there who want to hurt kids," Papi said.

"Why do people want to hurt kids, Papi?" I asked.

"'Cause they are crazy," Bobby said.

"Not everyone is a good person, Nina. You kids have to promise me that you will stay away from strangers," Papi pleaded.

"I promise," Bobby said.

"Me too," I said.

The police never found the man who tried to kidnap me at the school yard. And to protect the students, the principal kept all students inside during recess. No kids were allowed to play in the school yard for the rest of the school year.

17

Last Day of School.
June 1969.

Our last day of school was warm, sunny, and beautiful. We were happy to be out for the summer. The students went to class in the morning, cleaned out their desks, and by noon everyone was dismissed. Sara, Blanca, Millie, Miguel, and I walked home from school.

"Hey, let's get some egg creams," I suggested.

"Yeah, let's get some!" Sara said.

We walked into the candy store on the corner of Hooper and South 2nd Street. Millie, Miguel, and Blanca looked around the store as Sara and I ordered our favorite soda fountain drink.

"Two egg creams, one vanilla and one chocolate," I said.

"Two egg creams coming right up," the owner said.

We loved egg creams. Sara and I watched as the owner blended melted ice cream, chocolate syrup, and pressurized seltzer water, then poured it into one large glass. We knew that we could only find this fountain drink in candy stores and only in Brooklyn.

"Yum," Sara said as she watched the man make each egg cream.

"Delicious," I said.

"Fifteen cents each," said the attendant.

I dug my hand in my pocket and pulled out a dime.

"Millie, do you have a nickel?" I asked. "I'll share my egg cream with you."

"Yeah, I do. I don't want anything else anyway," Millie said.

Blanca had a quarter and made sure she let the kids know about it. She didn't order anything. Miguel was broke as usual.

"Sara, can I have some of your egg cream?" asked Miguel.

"Sure!" said Sara. "Take a sip."

We left the store and happily shared our drinks.

"Let's play a game of stick ball when we get home," Miguel said.

"I can't," I said. "I have to go to the babysitter and wait for Mami to get home."

"Oh, come on," Blanca said. "Just for a little bit. We can have a quick game."

It didn't take much to convince me to play. I loved playing stickball just as much as I loved jumping Double Dutch. As soon as we got to the apartment building, we dropped our book bags on the stoop and quickly took our positions on our make-believe plates.

I was the first batter up. I held the broomstick in my hand, rolled the ball off the bat, let it bounce, and whacked it. I had such finesse. I hit the ball so hard, it had home run written all over it.

"Come on, Nina, run!" Sara said.

I scored. I made it to home plate with no problems and Miguel was still looking for the ball.

"Give me five," said Sara.

About an hour went by. It was time for me to bat again when I turned around and saw Carmen standing behind me. Carmen gave me a stern look and I quickly dropped the broomstick.

"What are you doing? You are supposed to be inside," Carmen said.

I looked at her and put my head down like I knew I was wrong. I walked to the stoop, picked up my book bag and waved goodbye to my friends. I walked inside the apartment building while Carmen walked right behind me.

"I'm sorry Carmen, I should have come here right from school," I said.

"That's okay Nina. I was worried. I'm glad you're okay," she said as she gave me a hug.

18

Summer Time. 1969.

My summer routine was pretty much the same every day. I was nine years old and still going down to my babysitter by 8 a.m. every morning and staying there until Mami picked me up at 4 p.m. I spent most of my day coloring, writing in my notebook, and watching TV. Some mornings I would go to the bodega with Carmen to pick up fruit and bread.

One rainy morning, I was coloring in my coloring book when someone knocked on Carmen's door. Carmen looked through the peephole and sighed. She put the chain on and then opened the door. It was her son, whom she hadn't seen for years.

"What do you want?" Carmen asked.

"Mami, let me in. I need a place to stay," he said.

"Where have you been, Tito?" she asked.

"I've been around. Please let me in," he said.

Carmen removed the chain and opened the door to let Tito in. From where I was sitting in the living room, I was able to see how dirty he looked. He had greasy long hair, a beard, and wore faded jeans. His white T-shirt had stains all

over it. Tito looked like he had the sniffles. His eyes were red
and watery.

"I'm sick," he said.

"Sick how?" Carmen asked sarcastically. "I told you to get
help."

"Not like that ma!" Tito said. "I'm clean. I've been clean
now for ten months; please believe me!"

I looked at Tito and then back down at my coloring book,
pretending that I was coloring. *He looks dirty*, I thought.

"Go take a bath and put on some clean clothes," Carmen
said.

"Do I still have my old room?" Tito asked.

"Yeah, and your clothes too," Carmen said.

I kept my head down as Tito walked by me. He gave me
the creeps. Yuck! He smelled bad too.

"Who's this?" he asked.

"She is the girl from upstairs. I babysit her every day,"
Carmen answered. "Go to the bathroom!"

Tito went in his bedroom, picked up a towel and some
shorts, and got in the shower. Meanwhile, I watched TV and
Carmen began to cook. Soon after Tito was finished with his
shower, he walked through the kitchen wearing only boxer
shorts.

"Put some clothes on right away," Carmen said. "We have
a little girl here."

"Okay, ma, don't freak out!" he said.

Tito walked past me and went straight into his room. I

pretended that I didn't see him. I just kept coloring and watching TV.

~

An hour or so went by, and Carmen finished making chicken soup, asopao. She called me to the table to eat. Tito must have fallen asleep in his room.

"Smells delicious," I said. "I like to eat this. Mami makes it all the time."

I had just finished eating my entire bowl of the thick chicken stew when I heard a knock on the door. Carmen looked through the peephole. It was my mother.

"Lydia, come in. Nina just got done eating," Carmen said.

"¿Como esta mi hija?" Mami asked.

"Bien Mami," I said as I hugged her.

"Gracias, Carmen," Mami said.

I picked up my stuff and left with my mother. I couldn't wait to go outside and play. Carmen was nice and she took good care of me, but she never let me go outside to play.

"Nina, I'm sorry, but I am responsible for you," Carmen once told me. "You can go out when your mother comes home and gives you permission."

19

Curious

I was down in Carmen's apartment the next morning by 7:50 a.m. It had been raining all night and it appeared as though the rain would continue all day. The air was hot and muggy; gray clouds were piled up like giant rocks. *Another rainy day*, I thought. *Bor-ing*. I knew I wouldn't be able to go out to play today because of the rain. I lay on the sofa and fell asleep.

I woke up around 10 a.m. starving. I went to the kitchen and poured myself a bowl of Corn Flakes and milk. I sat down at the table next to the window hoping to get some fresh, cool air. No such luck. It was too warm outside. Carmen was at the sink washing dishes.

"Nina, I have to go across the street to the bodega to buy some ham and cheese for lunch today. It's raining outside, so just sit in the living room and watch TV until I get back," Carmen said. "Okay? Tito is sleeping in his room. He won't bother you and I will be quick."

"Okay," I responded.

I ate my cereal and went back into the living room to watch television. There wasn't much to see. The cartoons normally started in the afternoon. I was really bored.

"I'm leaving now," Carmen said. "I'll be right back."

"Okay," I said.

I heard Carmen open and close the front door. I picked up my coloring book and began to color. I remember hearing a song the night before while sitting on my fire escape. I couldn't get it out of my head. I started humming and singing, *"Hey Jude, don't make it bad. Take a sad song and make it better. Remember to let her into your heart. Then you can start to make it better."* That was all that I remembered, so I kept repeating the verse over and over again.

Tito opened the door to his room, "Will you be quiet! I'm trying to sleep," he said.

I flinched when I heard his voice. He startled me. I was scared to say anything. Within minutes, I smelled a strange odor coming from his room. I had never smelled a scent like that before. He was burning something. I became curious. Tito's door was slightly open. I wanted to peek to see what was going on, but I hesitated and kept coloring.

The smell got worse. I slid off the sofa, tiptoed over and peeked through the door. Tito was sitting up on his bed smoking what looked like a cigarette. It smelled kind of funny, almost like the dead skunk my father ran over when we drove to the lake the other day.

I watched as he took a deep puff and inhaled it. He closed his eyes as he held his breath for a few seconds. He looked like he was enjoying it. The smell got to me. I couldn't stand it. As

I took a step back, the door opened accidently. Tito looked at me furiously.

"What are you doing?" he asked.

I stepped back into the living room. Tito began to walk toward me. He eyes were glaring as he looked down at me, pounding his fist in his other hand. My face turned white as a ghost and I began to shiver. I was so scared. He looked like he was getting ready to hit me.

Within seconds, we heard someone fumbling with keys and trying to unlock the front door. Tito stopped in his tracks and ran into his room. He closed the door. I took a deep breath and felt a sense of relief when I saw Carmen walk through the front door. I walked over to hug her. Carmen immediately smelled the weird scent in her apartment. She recognized it.

"Nina, are you all right?" Carmen asked.

"Yeah, I'm okay Carmen," I said.

Carmen put her purse and grocery bags on the table. She walked over to Tito's room and began to bang on his door.

"What are you doing in there? You lied to me! Get out of my house now!" Carmen yelled.

Tito opened the door.

"Ma, relax!" Tito said.

"No, I can go to jail for this. You shouldn't be here. Get out of here! You're going to get me in trouble!" Carmen yelled. "Get out! Get out now!"

"All right now!" Tito yelled back. "Calm down."

Tito walked back into his room, picked up his stuff, and

packed some clothing in a bag. He walked toward his mother and came face to face with her. He jabbed a finger in her face and then quickly walked away. Carmen stared him down as she tried to control her anger. Tito saw Carmen's purse on the kitchen table and before he walked out the front door, he grabbed Carmen's wallet, opened it, and took her money. He looked at her like *this is what you get!* Carmen looked at him in disbelief. Then Tito walked out the door.

Carmen locked the door as soon as he left. When she turned around, she saw me sitting on the sofa with my knees curled up. She knew that I was scared.

"I'm sorry, Nina. I'm so sorry," Carmen cried as she kneeled in front of me and stroked my hair.

"It's okay, Carmen. Don't cry," I said.

I just couldn't understand how a son could treat his mother like that. Carmen was so nice! I would never treat my parents that way or steal from them. Later that evening, when Mami came to pick me up from Carmen's house, Carmen told her what had happened.

"Are you sure he is not coming back?" Mami asked. "I don't want to put my daughter through that again."

"No, Lydia. I know him. He won't come back," Carmen said.

20

That Evening

My parents, Bobby, and I were sitting down eating rice and beans and fried chicken.

"When I grow up, I'm going to get a nice yellow Corvette with stripes on it," Bobby said. "It's going to look real nice."

"You are going to give me a ride in it, right Bobby?" I asked.

"No! It'll be my car," he said.

"You're not very nice," I said.

"Bobby, you're going to have to work hard to get that car, but I know you can do it," Mami said.

"Yeah, anything is possible," Papi said. "I know that I had to work hard to buy my Chevy," Papi said.

"Can I have your car when I grow up?" Bobby asked excitedly. "I'll buy it from you."

"How are you going to pay for it?" I asked, waving my head back and forth.

"I'm going to be an architect when I grow up," Bobby said. "I'll be able to buy my own my Corvette, too!"

"What's an ar-chi-tect?" I asked, looking right into his

eyes.

"Someone who draws pictures of buildings," Bobby said, looking right at me like he knew what he was talking about.

"It's good to have dreams like that, Bobby," Papi said. "If I still have my car by the time you become an architect, you can keep it, hijo."

"I'm going to be a doctor when I grow up. I'm going to take care of all of you," I said.

"That is so nice of you, hija," Papi said.

Mami smiled at me. She then began to tell Papi about what had happened at Carmen's house. I could see the anger on my father's face. His eyes were wide open and his face was red.

"I don't want my daughter in that house anymore," Papi said.

"I know," Mami said. "I'm going to talk to Mamá to see if she can watch Nina. She already watches Bobby. I just don't want Nina and Bobby to fight in front of her. Mamá wouldn't be able to handle it. She's getting too old."

My grandmother, Mamá, had just moved next door to us in apartment number 21. She wanted to be close to Mami. Mamá was very strict.

"We'll talk to her tonight. I really don't want Nina at Carmen's house anymore," Papi said.

I wanted to say something. I wanted to tell my father that I would be okay with Carmen, that she would protect me. But I knew that Papi was already very angry. *Staying with grandma while Mami worked wouldn't be so bad*, I thought.

~

Shortly after dinner, the phone rang. It was my mother's brother, Tio Jesús, from Puerto Rico.

"Lydia, Doña Angelica died today. We are going to bury her on Friday," Tio Jesús said.

Doña Angelica was my mother's oldest stepsister. She had cancer in her stomach. Mami knew that her stepsister was going to die soon.

"Okay, we will try to fly down tomorrow or Thursday," Mami said. "It depends on how fast we get our airplane tickets."

"Good, we will be expecting you," Tio Jesús said.

"Bye," Mami said.

After hanging up the phone, Mami took a deep breath. She had tears in her eyes when she started to tell us about her stepsister.

"We have to fly to Puerto Rico. She is going to be buried on Friday," Mami said.

"I'm going to Puerto Rico?" I asked.

Mami looked at Papi.

"No, Nina, me and your mother are going to Puerto Rico. You are going to stay here," Papi said.

"By myself?" I asked.

"No Nina. You can stay with my sister, Tia Josephina, and Bobby can stay with Mamá," Mami said.

21

Tia Josephina. August 1969.

Tia Josephina lived in the Bay Ridge section of Brooklyn. She was a widow and had two daughters: Anita, who was older than me by one year, and Rosa, who was nine just like me. Tia Josephina's husband had drowned in the ocean after falling off a boat a few years prior. She was never quite the same after his death. Although she devoted herself to church and her religion, she was poor and couldn't afford to buy plane tickets to attend the funeral in Puerto Rico.

"Nina is a good girl, but if you have to discipline her, go right ahead. You have my permission," Mami said. "We'll be back next Friday."

"Don't worry. She'll be fine," Tia Josephina assured Mami in Spanish.

"Take care of my daughter, please," Papi said.

"I will; go with God," Josephina said sweetly.

Tia Josephina had green eyes and long blonde hair with strands of gray on top. Thin and nervous at times, her plain, pale skin, and lines around her forehead and eyes made her look ten years older. She had long painted fingernails and her oversized button-down shirt, long ruffled skirt, and flat sandals made her look like a bag lady on the streets of New York City.

Mami and Papi had just left and it was still early in the afternoon. The girls had not changed since I last saw them at Bobby's Halloween birthday party three years earlier. Anita, the oldest daughter, had green eyes and long light-colored hair like her mother. A little taller than me and barefooted, Anita wore a long sleeve shirt and pants. Looking a lot like me, Rosa had long dark hair and eyes, as well as my skin color and height. Like her sister, she wore a long sleeve shirt and pants that were a little too warm for the month of August.

Anita and Rosa tried to make me feel at home. They took me to their bedroom and showed me where I would sleep. They had bunk beds. Anita slept on top and Rosa slept on the bottom. I would be sleeping with Rosa on the lower bed. The girls taught me how to play all sorts of games. I was excited to finally learn how to play Jacks and use a Hula Hoop. At night we talked a lot and played their Mystery Date board game.

Playing Mystery Date made me think about boys in a way that I never did before. I started to really wonder what it would be like to go on a date. I knew that my parents would never allow me to have a real boyfriend, so it was nice to pretend to have one. During the game, I kept my fingers crossed and hoped for the cute boy who wore the nice suit.

My first day at Tia Josephina's was great. The girls and I

were having a great time. We laughed at our funny jokes and riddles. However, I was not prepared for the living hell that I was about to go through.

~

After waking up the next morning, my cousins and I were playing in the bedroom when Tia Josephina came in yelling. Her face was red as she pulled back her lips and bared her yellow teeth.

"We have work to do!" she said. "Stop playing and start cleaning, all of you."

The girls jumped up and cleaned their room as fast as they could. I tried to help.

"Nina, go wash dishes while Rosa mops the floor," Anita said. "I'll clean the bathroom."

I had never washed a dish in my life. At home, all I had to do was make sure that my Castro Convertible bed was put away and that the living room was clean. However, I was willing to help my cousins. I walked over to the sink, turned on the water, and picked up the dishcloth. I took the dish washing liquid, poured almost the entire thing on the dishcloth, and poured some into the sink. I picked up a dish and started to wash it. I had trouble rinsing it, maybe because I had used too much soap. There were bubbles everywhere. It reminded me of my bubble baths. The bubbles began to overflow onto the floor.

"Nina, stop," Anita said. "Haven't you ever washed dishes before?"

"No," I laughed out loud.

Tia Josephina heard Anita. She walked into the kitchen and saw us by the sink.

"What the hell are you girls doing? Look at the mess you made!" Tia Josephina screamed.

She quickly approached us and grabbed us by the hair. She smacked Anita on the face and spanked my behind with her hand. Anita and I started crying. I was terrified.

"Clean up this mess now!" yelled Tia Josephina.

Rosa came in and wiped the floor clean. Anita finished washing dishes while I dried them. Tia Josephina supervised us as we cleaned up.

"Now go to your room and stay there!" she yelled.

I had no idea that my cousins were being treated just like my friend Miguel. Anita and Rosa told me that they were beaten on a daily basis. No wonder they always wore long sleeve shirts and long pants. They had to cover up their bruises and welts. It didn't take long before I also got my share of the beatings. Tia used whatever she got her hands on; belts, extension cords, and hangers were her favorites. She hated to hit us with her hands for fear that she would break one of her fingernails. She would line us up and beat us one by one. My cousins were so used to the beatings that they would stay still with their eyes closed and cry as their mother whipped them. I, on the other hand, always tried to escape. I would hide underneath the bed. Tia would always find me.

"Get out of there now!" she yelled. "I'm going to get you!"

"I want my Papi!" I would cry out. I could feel my body trembling and the sweat pouring down my back. I covered my face and squeezed my eyes shut. I cried uncontrollably.

"Your Papi isn't here," Tia said, as she swung her belt and hit me on my leg. She just kept swinging and swinging.

~

It was Thursday evening, the night before my parents were scheduled to come back from Puerto Rico. Anita, Rosa, and I were sitting outside on the stoop when two boys stopped by to talk to us. Hector and Lorenzo went to school with Anita and Rosa. Hector was skinny and dark-skinned with kinky hair and white teeth. He looked about Anita's age. Lorenzo had light brown skin, blond curly hair, and was kind of chunky. He was closer to my age.

"This is my cousin Nina," Anita said. "Nina, this is Hector and that's Lorenzo."

"Hi," I said blushing. I thought the boys were cute. Hector had a nice smile and Lorenzo had nice dimples.

"Hi," replied the boys as they waved.

"Nina, these boys are so funny. Wait until you hear their jokes," Anita said.

"What jokes?" Hector asked with a smirk on his face.

"Yeah, what jokes?" Lorenzo said as he winked at Anita.

The boys looked at us and began to crack jokes.

"Why was six afraid of seven?" Lorenzo asked.

"I don't know," I said.

"Because seven eight nine," Lorenzo said making a funny face.

"Ha ha," we chuckled.

"Here's one," Hector said. "Knock, knock."

"Who's there?" Anita asked.

"Lettuce," Hector said.

"Lettuce who?" Rosa asked.

"Lettuce in, it's freezing out here," Hector said in a loud funny voice.

The boys made all kinds of strange faces, too. Lorenzo made a face like Laurel from *The Laurel and Hardy Show* and he looked just like him. He also showed us his coin trick where he magically made a coin disappear. Hector showed us some of his card tricks. We were having a good time. We burst into laughter. They were so funny.

All of a sudden, we heard the door open behind us. We looked back and there she was. Tia Josephina was standing there, staring us down. Her hands clenched and unclenched as she held a belt in her right hand. I could see her nostrils flaring, muscles and veins straining against her skin. Tia kicked the door wide open.

"Get in here, now!"

Anita and Rosa got up and started to go up the stoop. Tia started beating them in front of the boys. The boys looked at each other and ran down the street as the girls cried. I managed to run past the girls into the house, untouched by Tia's belt. Once again, I hid under the bed in the girls' room.

Tia came after me. "Nina, get out of there right now!"

I refused to move or say anything. I lay under the bed with my knees to my chest and covered my face. Tia just kept swinging the belt under the bed hoping to hit me. She managed to whip me a couple of times on my arms and legs.

Finally, Tia Josephina gave up and went to bed. I came out as soon as I noticed that Tia was out of sight. Rosa and Anita were still crying in their beds.

"I have to get out of here," I said.

"You can't leave," Anita said. "My mother will find you and she'll beat you again."

"I'm jumping out this window and I'm never coming back," I said.

"You can't; you will die. We are on the second floor," Rosa said.

I looked out the window. It seemed a little high to jump safely.

"I have an idea. I'll use this sheet as a rope. Anita, you and Rosa hold on to this end and I'll hold on to the other end. Just don't let go. Okay?" I said.

Anita agreed. She held her end and I took hold of my end. I straddled the windowsill first. I looked down and then looked at the girls.

"Please don't let go," I pleaded.

"We won't," Anita promised.

I began my journey down the window. I held on to the sheet as tight as I could. I was now in front of the first floor window.

"Almost there," I yelled.

I looked up and couldn't see Anita or Rosa. Before I knew it, I was falling down into the exterior entryway to the cellar of the building. I hit my head against the concrete stairwell and was knocked unconscious. Blood poured out from the back of my head.

According to Rosa, Tia Josephina walked in on them as they were holding the sheet; they got scared and let go. When Tia looked down and saw me unconscious, she began to scream and cry hysterically. She thought I was dead. I was still unconscious when the ambulance arrived.

"What happened?" the ambulance attendant asked Tia.

"I don't know," said Tia. "I was sleeping."

"Are you her mother?" the attendant asked.

"No, I'm her aunt. Her mother is coming back from Puerto Rico tomorrow," answered Tia.

"We're going to have to take her to the hospital," the attendant told Tia. We need her guardian to come with us."

"Okay, I'll come," Tia said.

~

I awoke the next day in Kings County Hospital in Brooklyn. It felt very foggy to me but I was able to see a doctor and a nurse reapply some kind of bandage on my head. The nurse held my head as the doctor wrapped it completely with the bandage. I thought I was dreaming. I tried to sit up. I raised my pant leg up and saw a big welt on my right calf. I then realized that it was not a dream after all.

"What happened to you? Who did that to you?" the nurse asked.

"I don't know," I said as I rested back in bed. I closed my eyes and immediately fell asleep.

By the time I woke up again, I was back home in my apartment on South 2nd Street. Mami and Papi were sitting right next to me along with Bobby.

"Mi hija," Mami cried.

"How do you feel, Nina?" Papi asked.

I tried to sit up to hug my parents. I was so happy to see them, but was too weak to move. My parents hugged me. As days went by, I became stronger and stronger. By the end of the week, I was walking again. A few days later, I had my bandage and stitches removed. I noticed a bald spot on my head right where the stitches were. I had to wear a hat every day for the next few weeks until my hair grew back in. I didn't want anyone to see my bald spot.

I never told my parents what happened at Tia Josephina's house. But by the way they behaved, they already knew. One morning, I overheard a conversation between my mother and grandma, Mamá.

"I grabbed her and smacked her face. I never gave her permission to hit Nina," Mami said. "I kicked her ass. I never want to see Josephina again. I don't care if she is my sister."

Mamá was speechless. She didn't like to see her daughters fight, but deep down inside, she knew that Tia Josephina deserved what she got. I never saw Tia Josephina in person again, but I did have nightmares of her beatings for weeks. I also worried about my cousins and prayed that Anita and Rosa would be all right.

22

The Bird

The first day of school felt great to me. Everything seemed normal. I got to see my old friends and I loved the idea that I was now in fifth grade. To make it even better, Mami was no longer working. The factory where she worked ran out of business and she was okay with that. She was able to collect unemployment. I think she also may have felt guilty about what happened to me at Tia Josephina's house and wanted to be home to provide Bobby and me a sense of security.

After dismissal from school one afternoon, I walked home and ran up the stairway of my apartment building. I was excited to come home to Mami. I felt safe around my mother and I knew that she would always have something for me to eat when I got home from school. As I climbed up the stairs, I heard a familiar sound. I slowed down and listened carefully to what I was hearing. *It's that bird again*, I thought. I used to hear the bird all the time whenever I got home from school.

I walked to my apartment and knocked on my door. Mami opened it. By this time, the bird was quiet. I walked up to Mami and asked her a question.

"Mami, what does *pendejo* mean?" I asked so innocently.

"What? Where did you hear that word?" she asked. Her eyes widened.

"Mami, I heard the bird say it," I said.

"What bird?" Mami asked.

I ran to the small bedroom window facing the back yard and pointed to a window across from our apartment. There was a birdcage on the windowsill and inside was a big, colorful talking bird with green feathery wings and tail. It had a yellow face and head and a curved, black beak.

"That bird," I said.

Mami opened our window to listen to the bird. Sure enough, it was cursing up a storm.

"Pendejo, pendejo, pendejo, pendejo," sang the bird. He was non-stop.

Mami's eyes squinted as she stared at the bird, her posture stiffened for a moment. She spread her fingers out in a fan against her chest. It was obvious that she had never heard or seen that bird before. She instantly closed the window and in a high pitched voice, she began to speak.

"Don't listen to him," Mami said. "Keep this window closed."

"But Mami, I hear him every day. I can hear him in the hallway," I said.

"Nina, he is saying a bad word and I don't want you to repeat it, okay?" Mami said.

"Okay, Mami," I said.

I found out later that the true meaning of *pendejo* is *pubic hair*. However, it is considered a Spanish profanity, which varies in Spanish-speaking nations. In Puerto Rico, it has different meanings depending on the situation. It can range from *dummy* to just plain *idiot*. I remember clearly the first time I heard the word. Tia Josephina used to call her daughters and me *pendejas* all the time. She never really called us by our real names.

I didn't dare to tell my mother about all of the names that Tia Josephina used to call me. I knew that if I did, Mami would become angry. I didn't want to cause any more trouble in the family and I didn't want the memories back either.

23

Nina the Author. 1969.

I enjoyed fifth grade a lot. I had a great reading teacher who encouraged me to read and write; her name was Mrs. Susskind. Tall and thin with light brown eyes that gleamed, Mrs. Susskind had a pale complexion, a beautiful smile, and a nice clear voice. Responsible for the school's book fair, Mrs. Susskind held the fair every year in the library. She gave her students reading and writing assignments all the time. One of the assignments was writing books.

Upon writing the assignment on the board, Mrs. Susskind reviewed her guidelines with all of her students. Each student had to come up with his or her own story. They were to create their own illustrations as well. The book had to have a cover page. Mrs. Susskind encouraged us students to write as much as we wanted.

I loved the idea of writing a book. It was as though a light bulb lit up in my head. I had many ideas. *I'll write about a tall man,* I thought. I began to write my story. The story line came natural to me. I drew my own pictures for the book. I took construction paper, cut it to size, and wrote my story. I created a cover page and to make it thicker, I glued one piece of construction paper on top of another. I numbered each page and then stapled everything together. The cover page had a drawing of a tall man with a hat. The book's name was *The Tall Man,* written by Nina Inez Tavarez.

My book was finished in time for the book fair the next day. It sold for five cents that very same day.

"I can't believe it! I sold my first book real fast," I told my parents. "I need to keep writing so that I can make more money."

Mami and Papi looked at each other and smiled.

"That's good Nina. I am so proud of you," Papi said.

"Me too," Mami said.

"What are you going to write about next?" Bobby asked.

I looked at Bobby.

"Let me see... Oh, I know—a story about the chubby man," I said with a smirk on my face.

Bobby gave me a dirty look. I went to the living room and began to write my new book. By the end of the night I was done with book number two.

~

"Mrs. Susskind, Mrs. Susskind, I have a new book," I said the next morning upon arriving to her class.

"That's great, Nina. I will drop it off at the book fair this morning," Mrs. Susskind said.

My book sold before the end of the school day. Mrs. Susskind was so excited for me. She couldn't wait to tell me.

"Nina, your book sold today already," Mrs. Susskind said. "Here's your nickel."

I jumped up and down with joy.

"I can't believe it! I'm going to go home and write more books," I said.

By the end of the month, I had written ten books, all of which sold right away. My friends were happy for me, but a few of my classmates envied me. There was one girl in particular who hated me: Sonia Osorio.

24

Here Comes Trouble.
October 1969.

Sonia Osorio had hated me since first grade for many reasons. She always thought that I was a teacher's pet. She hated that I was popular in school and prettier than she was, or at least that's what the boys used to tell me. However, Wilbert Hernandez was the real reason why Sonia hated me. Sonia had a crush on Will since kindergarten. She'd known him longer than I had, but Will had a crush on me since first grade and I liked him. Will was my height, with light skin, medium brown wavy hair, and dark eyes. He was quiet and sometimes came across as being shy. It was in third grade when Will finally had the guts to ask me to be his girlfriend. As he was standing in the cafeteria line, Will asked me the question.

"Do you want to be my girlfriend, Nina?"

I hesitated to answer him. I knew that I liked him since first grade, but I never had a boyfriend before.

"Okay," I responded.

As soon as I said yes, our classmates began chanting.

"Nina and Will, Nina and Will," they sang.

They were so happy for us. Will and I walked to the

cafeteria together, sat at a table, and blushed as we ate our lunch. We never said a word to each other.

Sonia became furious when she heard the crowd chanting. She passed by our table and looked at me with those glaring eyes. If looks could kill! Sonia, who was a little taller than me and heavier by a few pounds, had short brown hair and brown eyes. She never smiled and always looked like she was mad at the world.

One day after lunch, I got up from the lunch table, waved goodbye to Will, and walked out to the hall. Sonia was standing by the doorway and came face-to-face with me.

"So, you are Will's girlfriend now, aren't you?" Sonia said.

My heart sank when I saw her. I was afraid of her. Shaking, I tried to walk away but Sonia blocked me. I looked at Sonia's eyes and fear overtook me. I felt helpless. A teacher standing by the door sensed the tension and immediately began to yell at us.

"Get going, girls!" the teacher said.

Sonia and I started moving in different directions, but before we went our separate ways, she turned around and said, "I'm going to get you one day." I trembled at the sound of her voice. I had never had a problem with anyone, but Sonia really scared me.

All through third, fourth, and fifth grades, Sonia terrorized me. I tried to control my fear and show Sonia that I was not afraid of her. But if I saw her coming my way in the hall, I would turn around and walk all around the school to get to my classrooms. I avoided Sonia as much as I could. She wanted me to break up with Will. She wanted him all to herself, even though Will didn't want anything to do with her.

Whenever Sonia approached Will to talk to him, he would just walk away from her. She knew how much Will liked me. Will and I were more like friends who really liked each other. I never went out on an actual date with him. In fact, he and I never saw each other after school. We never kissed. And yet, there was something special about our friendship.

~

I was in fifth grade now and Will and I were still together. We had become closer; we talked to each other more often and he carried my books every chance he got. As for Sonia... Well, she was another story. She continued to terrorize me every time she saw me.

One afternoon, I was in my classroom sitting in my seat in the fourth row. There were huge windows to the left of me. I loved looking out the window, just daydreaming about Will and me. We were getting closer. He was now walking me half-way home from school. I would dream about us walking in the park together, just talking and playing on the swing.

I suddenly snapped out of my daydream and turned my head toward the classroom door. I noticed Sonia standing outside my classroom. Our eyes met. Sonia put up three fingers and began to move her lips.

"Three o'clock! Outside today!"

I looked at Sonia and motioned back.

"Okay, I'll be there!"

I knew Sonia wanted to fight me. I was still very afraid of her, but I had become tired of her bullying. After the bell rang, I really didn't know what to do. I didn't want to fight Sonia. I thought about running to my teacher and telling her about the fight, but I held back. I didn't want the kids in school to call me a chicken. So I decided to look around the school for another exit, but there was only one way out. I closed my eyes and took a deep breath. I hoped that when I walked out, Sonia would not be there. *Maybe Sonia is bluffing,* I thought.

I took my time walking down the stairway leading to the main entrance. I opened one of the steel double doors and when I walked through the doors, a crowd of kids was already waiting for me. I looked around and there was Sonia, right in the middle of the crowd.

"Come down!" Sonia yelled as she pounded her fists against each other.

I saw her standing there and something came over me. My normally calm and happy self quickly changed. I was now filled with rage. You could see it in my face; my nostrils were flared and my eyes were flashing and narrowing into slits. I dropped my book bag on the steps, closed my hands into fists, and walked right up to Sonia. *Enough is enough*, I thought.

Sonia made the first move. She pushed me. I pushed her back. She swung at me and I ducked. I jumped on top of her and wrapped my arms around her neck. Sonia began pulling my hair. I swung her body around and she stumbled and fell. I got on top of her and straddled my legs around her waist, pinning her arms. She couldn't move. I began to hit Sonia in the face. I slapped her as much as I could. I even ripped off her blouse, exposing her training bra. I had completely lost control of myself.

Within minutes, the principal came running down the steps to break up the fight.

"Come on, break it up!" he shouted, pulling me off Sonia. "Nina, you are fighting?" He sounded surprised.

I looked at him and put my head down. I felt ashamed and disappointed.

"Go home, both of you," he said. "And if I hear of any more fighting, you will both be suspended."

We nodded. Sonia gathered her belongings and ran off. I picked up my book bag and began to walk home.

A crowd of kids walked right behind me, chanting my name. I was the champion of that fight with not a scratch on my face. I finally faced Sonia and overcame my fear of her. *She is nothing. I kicked her butt!* I thought. However, no matter how much I tried to convince myself that I had done the right thing by fighting Sonia, deep down inside I was not proud of myself. Fighting was not my thing. It was only an act of survival.

As I got closer to my apartment building, I saw Mami looking out the window. She saw the crowd of kids walking behind me. I turned around and said goodbye to my friends as

I ran upstairs to my apartment. Mami opened the door.

"¿Nina, que paso?" Mami asked.

I told my mother the whole story. I told her about Sonia and the bullying that I had faced every day at school. I even told Mami about Wilbert.

"Okay, Nina, I understand that you had to defend yourself. But next time someone starts something with you, let me know."

"All right Mami," I said.

"And Nina," she added.

"Yes Mami?"

"No boyfriend. You are too young," she said. "Your father wouldn't want you to have a boyfriend, either."

"Okay Mami," I said. I frowned when Mami wasn't looking.

~

Back in school the next morning, the principal met with Sonia and me and gave us a lecture about fighting. Neither one of us told the principal why we had fought.

"We won't fight again," Sonia said. She had a big bruise on her left cheek and some cuts on her forehead from the fight.

"Yeah, I don't want to fight anymore," I said.

After warning us about the consequences of fighting again, the principal asked for our word that we would never fight again. He then dismissed us. Sonia and I walked away from the principal's office. We didn't even look at each other.

After our meeting with the principal, Sonia and I never spoke to each other again. She avoided me altogether. And as for Will and me... well, we were no longer boyfriend and girl-friend. I told Will what my mother said, and Will was all right with that. We continued to sit together during lunch in the school's cafeteria, but only as friends.

25

Crawling Creatures.
Spring 1970.

At the age of ten I had beautiful, long brown hair that I parted down the center. It was thick and silky. There were days when I would tie my hair into a ponytail and other days when I would let it hang loose. People complimented me on my hair all the time. I loved it and now I was faced with cutting it.

"Nina, we have to cut your hair short," Mami said.

"But, Mami, I like my long hair," I protested as I scratched my head.

I knew that Mami was right. Quite honestly, I couldn't stand the itching any more. One glimpse of my hairbrush was all it took for me to agree to get my hair cut short. I screamed when I saw the nasty, tiny, wingless bug on my brush. I hated the thought that something was crawling on my head. I couldn't stop scratching and the itchiness was even worse at night.

I had been complaining for days that something was moving around on my head. After one look at my scalp, Mami knew exactly what I was dealing with. She saw tons of nits on my hair. Boy, were they hard to get off; they were almost glued to my hair.

"I knew it," Mami said. "Tienes piojos, you have lice."

"I have piojos?" I asked.

"Si, I told you not to get too close to Millie," Mami said. "Esa es una piojosa! Her head is filled with lice."

"How do you know that, Mami?" I asked.

"Our neighbor, Doña Maria told me. She saw them in Millie's hair," Mami said.

"Mami, I'm afraid. What if they stay with me forever?" I asked.

"Nina, don't worry," Mami assured me. "Your Tia Blanca will take care of it. She's a beautician and she knows what to do. She'll give you a nice haircut tonight."

~

Tia Blanca came over. Resembling Tia Josephina somewhat, my Tia Blanca had long blonde hair and green eyes with nice thick eyelashes. She was single and short with nice teeth and smooth skin, and she wore a different hair style practically every day. A hairdresser at night and on weekends, Tia Blanca was a bank teller during the day. As Mami's youngest sister, she was full of laughter and smiles. And she loved to shop.

"Okay Nina, are you ready for this?" Tia Blanca asked as I sat on a chair in the living room with no mirror in sight.

I closed my eyes and smiled, showing all of my teeth.

"Yeah, I'm ready. Go ahead," I said.

Tia Blanca wrapped a towel around my shoulders and took a pair of scissors from her purse. Cutting from the bottom up, Tia took off the length first and then began to cut the strands on top. I could hear the sound of the scissors snipping away as I watched fragments of long hair fall to the floor. Tia Blanca was fast.

"All done, Nina," she said. "We have to wash your hair now."

"Can I see first?" I asked.

"Sure," Tia said.

I ran to my mother's bedroom and looked in the mirror. Although I was surprised to see how short it was, Tia Blanca had really given me a cute boyish haircut. It really did feel good to me; I didn't have to worry about things crawling on my shoulders anymore.

After the haircut, Tia Blanca shampooed my hair with some medicated liquid to treat the lice. I felt better in a matter of days and before I knew it the itchiness was gone. My mother checked my head and confirmed that I didn't have any more lice.

Knowing how much I loved my long hair, Tia Blanca felt bad for cutting my hair and wanted to make it up to me. She came to visit me over the weekend and took me shopping. We shopped for clothes on Broadway Avenue. I always enjoyed my shopping sprees with Tia Blanca, as she spoiled me every chance she could. Tia bought me a few cute outfits. I loved my green sleeveless dress, blue shorts, and shirts. She had good taste. Afterward, we stopped by the ice cream shop and ate some delicious pistachio ice cream—my favorite! We stopped at the record store and she bought me my favorite 45-rpm record, "Band of Gold" by Freda Payne. I couldn't wait to go home and listen to it.

"Nina, are you having a nice time?" Tia Blanca asked.

"I'm having a great time!" I said.

Several hours later, Tia Blanca brought me back home. Mami was by the door when I came in. She could see that I was excited.

"Mami, Mami, look what Tia bought me!" I said with a huge smile.

"Are you spoiling my daughter again?" Mami smiled as she asked Tia.

"Nina is one of my favorite nieces. I love to buy her things," Tia Blanca said. "I have to go now. Bye, Nina."

"Bye, Tia. Thank you! I love you," I said as I gave her a hug and kissed her cheek.

After Tia Blanca left, I ran to the living room, lifted the lid of our record player, and played my new record. I sang along as I listened to the song. I pretended that I was Freda Payne singing "Band of Gold."

Since you've been gone all that's left is a band of gold
All that's left of the dreams I hold
Is a band of gold and the dream of what love could be

If you were still here with me...

It didn't take long for my hair to grow back. After several months, my hair was down to my shoulders again. Millie had also gotten a haircut, as did the rest of my girlfriends. I guess we were all loaded with those crawling creatures. I'm just glad we got rid of them.

26

Friends Forever

By the summer of 1971, at the age of eleven, I started to notice changes in my body. At four feet eleven inches tall, I weighed about one hundred pounds. My breasts got bigger and rounder, my hips got curvier, and my waist—well, it stayed little. I had my mother's guitar figure and I was okay with that. And just like my mother, I respected my body. *Nobody will see me naked*, I thought. When Mami asked to look at my breasts for bra sizes, I said no. Mami had to take me to the store in order for me to try on bras in the dressing room privately. Once I found the right size, I let my mother know.

The boys also noticed the changes in my body. They would always flirt with me whenever I walked past them. Sometimes their comments angered me. *Can't a girl wear whatever she wants without being looked at like that?* I thought.

Blanca, Sara and Millie were also experiencing physical changes. At my height, Blanca still had her round figure and big stomach. Her breasts were the largest of the four of us. Millie was the tallest and the skinniest. She had small breasts and hips. One day we noticed that her breasts looked really big. We found out later that Millie was stuffing her bra with toilet paper. We had been playing around when we saw the paper sticking out of her bra. Her face turned bright red. Blanca laughed out loud. Sara and I kept quiet; we didn't want to hurt Millie's feelings. Millie ran home, took out the toilet paper, and never stuffed her bra again. As for Sara—well, she practically stayed the same, though perhaps a little taller and curvier around the hips. Her breasts looked like they were still growing.

Since we all had long hair, we changed our hairstyles every day. Sometimes we let our hair down and just let it flow and other times we wrapped it in a pony tail or braids.

The girls and I were also into fashion. In the winter we wore turtle neck shirts with our bell-bottom jeans that flared out from the bottom of the calf. I even had a red maxi coat that I loved to wear. It was long and came down to my ankles. In the summer we wore tie-front button-down sleeveless shirts, hot pants that were super short shorts, and flat sandals or white go-go boots. We looked good! The girls loved when guys made flirty comments to them. They felt flattered. I felt the same way the girls did but only when the cute boys looked at me.

~

By now my parents were less strict with me. I was allowed to leave my block, go shopping on Broadway Avenue, and explore the rest of Williamsburg with my friends. I loved living here. I wasn't afraid of anything. I knew everyone. People were very friendly. But most importantly, I liked my freedom a lot. I was still daddy's little girl, but I felt more grown up.

"Come on, Nina. Let's go to the record store on Broadway Avenue. I want to buy the Archies' new record," Blanca said.

"Oh! Can I borrow the record?" I asked.

"Yeah, if you go with us," Blanca said.

The girls and I walked up to Broadway Avenue. We laughed and sang a few songs along the way. We were all dressed alike, just as we'd planned. We had called each other right before leaving the house to make sure that we were wearing matching outfits.

I began to hum "Sugar, Sugar" by the Archies and soon the girls began to recite the song:

Sugar, ah, honey, honey. You are my candy girl. And you got me wanting you.
Honey, ah, sugar, sugar. You are my candy girl. And you got me wanting you.

We were just girls, laughing and having fun. We even had a bubble gum contest where we had to blow and pop bubbles. The one who blew the biggest bubble and popped it without getting it all over their face was the winner. Sara always won. She could put two pieces of bubble gum in her mouth and blow two separate bubbles at a time. Boy, she was good. Happy to be together, we kept on walking and didn't really care who saw or heard us as we walked down the street.

As soon as we entered the discount record store, we heard the song "ABC" by The Jackson 5 playing. The store was full of energy. There were lots of people walking through the aisles looking for great music. Some were standing around just talking about the latest songs. Couples smiled as they picked out their favorite love songs. There were aisles of large and small vinyl records by the Beatles, Temptations, Elvis, Diana Ross, Marvin Gaye, and countless others. I could see guitars hanging on the walls. The store even sold phonographs just like my white, portable record player at home.

Blanca walked right up to the counter where the Archies' records were and picked up the 45 rpm vinyl record. Sara, Millie, and I followed Blanca to the register and waited for her to pay for the record. Excited to listen to the record, we walked out of the store and went back home.

"Let's go to my house," I said. "I have my own record player."

"Okay," Blanca said.

"Yeah," Millie and Sara agreed.

We arrived at my apartment and knocked on the door. Mami opened the door and, by the aroma, I could tell that she was starting to cook.

"Hola," Mami said with a smile.

"Hola, Mami," I said.

"Hola, Señora," the girls said.

We walked into the living room and the girls sat on the

sofa as I walked into Bobby's room to get my record player. I placed the record player on the floor and plugged it in. Blanca put the record on the turntable and as soon as the music started, we stood up and began to dance. We smiled as we snapped our fingers, bent our knees, and tapped our toes on the floor. Afterward, we sat around and listened to more music as we talked. Sara, Millie, and Blanca were my best friends. We promised each other that we would stay friends forever.

27

Moving Out of Williamsburg

By the fall of 1971, my parents decided to move out of Williamsburg. They made plans to move to the Bay Ridge section of Brooklyn into the apartment building where Tia Josephina lived. Tia Josephina had owned the building, but abandoned it to move to Puerto Rico with her daughters. She couldn't keep up with the expense of owning an apartment building. My parents were the only family members who were financially stable and willing to take over the building.

I was not happy about the move. It brought back too many bad memories of the beatings that I endured from Tia Josephina. It was bad enough that I had a nasty scar on the back of my head from when I fell out the two-story window. I also had to leave my best friends behind.

"I don't want to move there," I said. "I don't want to see that place again."

"Nina, it will be better for all of us. You will have your own room," Mami said.

My parents didn't want to hear what I had to say. They had already made up their minds. We were going to move to

Bay Ridge and into Tia Josephina's old apartment. They were adamant about that.

~

By the time October came around we were completely packed. While my parents loaded up the moving truck, I stepped out onto my fire escape for the last time. I sighed as I took my last, long look around my neighborhood. Holding back tears, I looked at the bodega across the street, the candy store at the corner, and Dr. Cohn's office up the street. I began to reminisce about all the good times that I had here. Memories of so many wonderful moments ran through my head.

I remembered when I first met Millie, Sara, and Blanca and how they taught me to jump rope. Boy, we laughed a lot. I remembered when I first learned how to play stickball and hopscotch. I remembered walking to school with my friends. I remembered coming home from school and stopping by the candy store to buy egg creams. *I will never forget how delicious they were. Those were the good old days,* I thought as my heart began to shrink. I felt some tightness across my chest. My heart was definitely broken. The thought of leaving my friends, school, and South 2nd Street was too painful for me.

I looked down and saw my friends sitting on my stoop. They weren't speaking to each other; they just sat quietly, turning their heads as though they were looking for someone. I went back in the apartment and ran down the stairs to talk to them.

"Hi guys," I said, cracking a smile.

"We are going to miss you, Nina," Millie said. Her eyes watered.

"I will miss you too!" Blanca said as she threw her arms around me.

"Nina, I will miss you so much," Sara said, fumbling her words and hugging me.

"We will see each other again," I said as I held back my tears.

Miguel came running up the street. He had a wide grin and eyes that sparkled. His dark brown hair was nicely groomed. Wearing only a T-shirt and jeans, I could see how much he had grown. He didn't look like the skinny little boy I met a few years ago in the hallway after being beaten by his father. Miguel was actually cute now and more grown up.

"Nina, Nina," Miguel said as he took a deep breath. "I'm going to miss you!"

I hugged him and choked up. I began to sniffle; tears ran down my face. It took all I had to control myself and not break down in front of my friends. I wanted to see my friends happy, not sad. So I took a deep breath and sucked it up.

I will miss you too, Miguel," I said. "Please be careful. Listen to your parents, please. Promise me."

"I promise, Nina. Don't worry about me," he said as he hugged me.

Papi pulled up in his car in front of us. Mami was already sitting in the front and Bobby in the back. One of Papi's friends was driving the moving truck to our new apartment. They were ready to leave now.

"Come on Nina, let's go now," Papi said.

I got in the back seat and waved goodbye to my friends. They waved back. The car started to move. I turned around and kept my tear-filled eyes on my friends until I could no longer see them. I took a deep breath and closed my eyes.

Papi looked through his rear view mirror as he was driving. He noticed how upset I was.

"Nina, you will make new friends. I promise."

28

Bay Ridge

Our three-bedroom apartment in Bay Ridge was big and all the rooms were freshly painted. I now had my own private bedroom and so did Bobby. My grandmother, Mamá, had also moved to the same apartment building. She moved into the first floor apartment with her son, Luis, and his daughter, Maribel. Luis was my uncle, my mother's brother. He was older than my mother by a couple of years. Maribel was about nine years old.

By Monday I was already enrolled in P.S. 1 elementary school. I was in sixth grade and already didn't like the school. The teachers were nice and the kids were friendly, but I missed my friends in Williamsburg. It was hard for me to make new friends. *There is no way that I am going to replace my old friends with new ones,* I thought.

On top of that, I began to have nightmares of Tia Josephina beating me again. I felt rage building up inside of me. I developed a bad attitude and began to fight in school. In less than a month, I had gotten suspended twice for fighting. If someone looked at me the wrong way, I would get in their face and push them. I also began to rebel against my parents. *It's their fault that I'm like this,* I thought. *We didn't have to move.*

~

One day while I was walking to school, I saw two girls from my third period class, China and Sandra. It was rare when they showed up to class. China was thin, my height, flat-chested, and had dark skin and slanted eyes. Her brown kinky hair was slicked back in a bun. Sandra was a little taller than China and me. She had a round figure with medium-sized breasts, long brown wavy hair tied back in a pony tail, and dark eyes.

"Hey, Nina, let's go shopping on 5th Avenue; I don't want to go to school today," China said.

"Yeah, we can go to that one clothing store and get some new clothes," Sandra said.

"How? We don't have money," I said.

"I have some," China said as she winked at Sandra.

"Okay, let's go," I said. I didn't feel like being in school anyway.

We went into a clothing store and looked around as though we were shopping for real. I saw some nice shirts. I picked the shirts off the rack, but then put them back. I didn't have any money to buy anything. I turned around and saw China take a sweater and put it in her book bag while Sandra served as a lookout. I couldn't believe my eyes. I had no idea that the girls were going to steal. I felt terrible.

We were getting ready to walk out of the store when the store manger stopped us. He took us to the back of the store and searched us. Thank goodness I had no merchandise on me. However, China did and we all got in trouble for that.

The manager kept us in the back room and called the police. When the police officer arrived, I began to feel sick in my stomach. The officer held a little notebook pad and a pencil. He began to ask us questions.

"Why aren't you girls in school?" he asked.

China and Sandra crossed their arms, rolled their eyes, and turned their faces away from the officer. I just put my head down. The officer raised his eyebrows and gave us a glassy stare. He began tapping his foot on the floor.

"What's your name? Where do you live?" he asked as he looked at the three of us.

"My name is Nina," I said as my voice quivered. By now I was shaking.

China and Sandra turned around and looked at me. They shook their heads in disbelief. The police officer stared them down.

Finally, after more questions and a little pressure on us, we willingly gave the officer all the information that he wanted. The officer spoke with the store manager, got some more information, and then filed a report. The officer proceeded to contact our parents and had us wait in the store until our parents arrived.

My heart started pounding in my chest when I saw the

look on my father's face. He didn't have that warm smile that I was used to seeing. He was angry. His chin was up high and I could see his body tensing. He had left work to come for me and that alone didn't make him happy. Even more so, he was extremely disappointed in me. I saw the hurt in his eyes as he broke eye contact with me.

I looked at my father with my puppy eyes and leaned into him. I tilted my head and placed it against his belly. I looked up at his eyes.

"Papi, I am sorry," I said as tears poured down my face. "I never wanted to hurt you."

I loved my father so much. To me he was my angel in disguise. I promised him that I would never play hooky or get in trouble again.

The police officer walked over to my father and me and gave us a yellow paper.

"Here is a copy of the report and your court date," the officer said.

"But my daughter didn't take anything," Papi said.

"No, but she was an accomplice and she also played hooky. That's truancy," the officer explained.

I held my hands to my face and started bawling.

"No, I don't want to go to jail," I said.

The officer walked up and kneeled in front of me.

"No, you're not going to jail," he said. "You and your father have to go to court and pay a fine. However, the next time you do something like this, you will go to jail. Do you understand, Nina?"

"Yes," I replied.

We said goodbye to the police officer. As we walked toward Papi's car, I turned around and saw that China and Sandra were still waiting for their parents to show up. I really didn't care about them. I just wanted to get out of there. Papi and I got in the car and he drove me to school. He signed me in at the office and went back to work. I made sure that I attended all of my classes thereafter.

~

Even though I kept my promise not to get in trouble any more, my parents realized that they had made the wrong decision to move to Bay Ridge. They knew that I was not happy living in Tia Josephina's old apartment. They felt that they had let me down. At the end of the school year, my parents gave up the apartment building to another family member and we moved to Jersey City.

29

I Promise Not To Tell.
Jersey City, New Jersey. Fall 1972.

I have always said that my father saved me from doing all the wrong things. While living in Bay Ridge, fighting, playing hooky, shoplifting, and all the things that get kids in trouble came my way. I could have continued to do all of those bad things, but I chose Papi instead. I couldn't stand the thought of ever hurting my father... or my mother. Moving from New York to New Jersey was a nice move. I liked downtown Jersey City. There was so much to do in this large city and even better, my cousins Leticia and Maritza lived around the corner.

Leticia and Maritza were the daughters of Tio Pablo, one of my mother's older brothers. He was married to a woman named Eva, who we called Tia Eva. Leticia was a year older than me. Like her mother, she had a creamy complexion, dark eyes, and short hair. Leticia was nice but a little too quiet and I never knew why. Maritza was my age and had long black hair, light complexion, dark eyes, and a few little bumps on her forehead—pimples, she called them. Maritza was funny. Just like her father, she knew how to make people laugh. I enjoyed getting together with her every chance I could.

Now twelve years old and in seventh grade, I really liked my new school and all of my new friends. I got involved in sports and made the basketball team. My parents began to trust me again and gave me more freedom.

That year, I became good friends with a girl named Brianna. She was my age and we both attended the same school. Brianna had long, blonde hair and green eyes. At four feet eleven-and-a-half inches, she was almost as tall as me. I was exactly five feet. Her figure was pretty much like mine, only her hips were smaller and her boobs were bigger. Brianna lived around the corner from me. She became my first close American friend. We would talk about all kinds of things, but I always felt that she was holding back some things. She seemed quite mature for her age. The way she talked about guys had me thinking.

One day Brianna told me that she had a crush on the crossing guard who stood on the corner of Grove Street. The man was an actual police officer, over the age of twenty for sure. She almost looked like she was in another world as she spoke in a sweet, soft voice describing every detail of his body. Shocked and confused, I began to wonder about Brianna; something was wrong. To me, the thought of falling for a man that age was disgusting.

One evening, we sat on one of the benches in the park and started talking about boys. That's when Brianna felt the need to confess something to me.

"I want to tell you something, Nina, but you have to

promise me that you won't tell anyone," Brianna said.

"I promise not to tell. I promise. Tell me," I pleaded.

"No, forget it. You won't understand," she said.

"Come on, please, please," I said.

"All right! Well the other night while I was taking a bath... my brother came into the bathroom," Brianna said.

"Which one?" I asked. I knew that she had an older brother and a little one.

"The good looking one, Charlie," Brianna said with a broad smile. "He is so cute. He's seventeen years old."

"What? What was he doing in your bathroom?" I asked, feeling uneasy.

"Well, Charlie and I have taken many baths together," Brianna said softly. There was a devilish look of mischief in her eyes. She sounded like she was in love with her brother. She then began to tell me every detail of her relationship with Charlie.

"That's your brother, yuck!" I said.

"We love each other," Brianna tried to explain in a defensive tone. "You just don't understand."

"I don't want to understand. That's wrong," I said.

"Charlie doesn't think it's wrong. He should know, he's older," Brianna said.

"Do your parents know?" I asked.

"No, my mother kicked my father out a long time ago. He doesn't live with us any more," she said. "And my mother works until eleven o'clock every night."

"Why did she kick your father out, Brianna?" I asked curiously.

Brianna's eyes grew dark as her facial expression changed. She brought her knees to her chest and went into her own little world, almost like she was in a trance.

"She saw him coming out of the bathroom one night while I was taking a bath," Brianna said. "My mother had no idea what my father had been doing to me all those nights she worked late—no idea! When she saw him coming out of the bathroom with just a towel wrapped around his waist, she screamed and threatened to call the police. My father left us and I never saw him again. That was when my brother Charlie said that he would always take care of me."

"Does your mother know about you and Charlie?" I asked.

"Of course not," she said. "Are you crazy? And I will never tell her."

"Why?" I pleaded.

"Because she will kick Charlie out just like she did my father," Brianna said. "My mother is selfish. She wants all the men to herself. That is why she kicked my father out. Deep down inside she hates me."

I really didn't know what else to say. I felt chills running up and down my spine. I cringed at the thought of Brianna and her brother doing things that only a married couple should do. I felt sick in my stomach. I covered my face with my hands in complete disbelief. *Her father? Her brother?* I thought. *Gross!* It got to the point where I couldn't take it anymore.

"Brianna, I have to go home now," I said.

"Why?" Brianna asked.

"It's getting late," I said.

"Nina, you better not tell anyone about this. My brother will kill me," Brianna said.

"I promised you that I wouldn't tell anyone. Don't worry about it," I said.

I walked home disgusted. Brianna's confession really bothered me. It was something that I could not imagine. I thought about my brother Bobby. I loved Bobby, but not in the same way that Brianna loved her brother. *There is supposed to be a strong bond between siblings, but not like Brianna and her brother,* I thought. Their relationship was just sickening and too much for me to handle.

I felt the need to talk to someone about Brianna, but I knew that I couldn't. I had made a promise to Brianna and I was pretty good at keeping promises. I saw a church on my way home from the park. I decided to stop in to say a prayer. I walked in, dipped my fingers into the bowl of holy water, and made the sign of the cross. I kneeled in front of a pew and recited the Our Father prayer. I then proceeded to pray for Brianna.

"She doesn't know any better, Lord," I pleaded. "Please help her."

I prayed some more and thanked God for giving me the parents and brother that I had. Afterward, I got up, went home, greeted my parents, and took a shower. I went to bed only to toss and turn all night long. I struggled to fall asleep.

The next morning, Brianna and I walked to school together.

"You know what you are doing is wrong," I said.

"My brother doesn't think so and neither do I. I love him," Brianna said. "You better not tell anyone, Nina! I will never talk to you again if you do."

"I won't tell anyone," I said. "I promised you that."

We approached the school and I saw my basketball coach standing by the door.

"Are you ready to play today, Nina?" Coach asked.

"I'm ready!" I said.

"I'll see you during recess," he said.

I walked right to my homeroom class and Brianna walked to hers.

~

Although I tried to avoid hanging out with Brianna during the rest of the school year, I really worried about her all the time. It took all I had to keep quiet. I thought about talking to the guidance counselor at school or even to my parents, but I couldn't break my promise to Brianna. And I didn't want to make Brianna's home life worse.

Whenever Brianna and I would run into each other, she would always invite me to hang out with her. I just couldn't process any more details about her relationship with her brother, so my response to her invitations was always the same.

"I'm sorry Brianna, but I have to study tonight."

I became involved with basketball and kept myself busy with schoolwork. I had my own goals and dreams to fulfill. I had great parents and I wanted to make them proud. I knew that I had to study hard if I wanted to become a doctor, a dream of mine since I was five years old. I always knew that I wanted to take care of my family and save their lives as well as save the lives of others. *One day, I will learn how to help people like my friend Brianna.*

30

First Job in a Small City.
Hoboken, New Jersey. 1973.

I finished seventh grade and soon after my last day of school, my parents decided to move again. This time we were moving to the downtown section of the City of Hoboken, less than one mile away from where we were living before. My parents didn't like our cramped apartment in Jersey City and they were paying too much money for rent.

Hoboken reminded me so much of Brooklyn. Walking on the streets of this small city was actually fun. I could see people playing dominoes in front of their brownstone apartment buildings. I could hear the hissing sounds of the busses when they stopped at every corner. I could cross the Observer Highway, a main street in Hoboken, and just like that, I was back in Jersey City visiting my cousins Leticia and Maritza. The Path train was conveniently located on Hudson Place, making it easy to travel from Hoboken to New York City. The breeze and smell of the Hudson River made Hoboken's waterfront a popular place for teenagers to hang out. And the smells of the hot dog stands were delicious.

Soon after our move to Hoboken, I enrolled in a summer

youth employment program and at the age of thirteen, I learned about the duties and responsibilities of a job. I took pride in cleaning Hoboken's junior high school and the park near the school. I made many friends along the way.

One of them was a boy my age named Eddie, who I met on my first day of work. He was assigned to work as my partner, which is how the summer program worked. The kids all worked in pairs, groups, or teams so that they could monitor and keep track of each other. Wearing a dark afro, Eddie was a little taller than me and very skinny. I could practically see his ribs through his white tank top. He had a light complexion, hazel eyes, and dimples. He was nice. I liked him, but not like *that*. I wasn't ready for boys yet.

~

By eleven o'clock on one hot summer morning, my friend Eddie and I were sweeping the park and picking up trash.

"Did you pick up the trash around the basketball court?" I asked, checking to make sure he was doing his job.

"I sure did," Eddie said.

"Then we are done!" I said.

"Yep," Eddie said as he took a deep breath. "What now, Nina?"

"I need to use the bathroom. Eddie, can you walk up to the school with me?"

"Me, why me?" he asked.

"Eddie, it's like a ghost town in there! Only a few people around and they're all in the office," I said. "I hate to go in there alone."

"All right, Nina. Let's go," Eddie said.

We walked into the school through the main entrance. The school did look like a ghost town, which was typical of most schools in the summer time. Eddie and I walked over to the girl's bathroom.

"Wait for me here, Eddie. Don't go anywhere," I said.

"Don't worry, I won't," Eddie said.

I opened the door and entered the bathroom. I walked to the stall that was farthest away from the entrance. I relieved myself, pulled up my pants, and washed my hands. I was lathering my hands when someone walked into the bathroom. A man in a green uniform startled me. He was tall, obese, and had close-cropped gray hair. His nose was shaped like the bill of a parrot and his pale wrinkled face reminded me of a grandfather. I noticed his green teeth as he grinned and walked towards me. I was frightened.

"What do you want?" I said as I took a step back.

He started talking to me in a foreign language, *Polish*, I thought. I couldn't understand him. As he got closer, I noticed the last name on his shirt; it started with the letter O and ended with *zinski*. I started to shake. Each time I took a step back, he took a step forward.

"Eddie!" I yelled. "Eddie!"

Although it only took a few moments for Eddie to run into

the bathroom, it felt like eternity to me. He looked at the man in the green uniform and then looked directly at me. He saw my pale face, and from the sound of my voice when I called his name he knew that I was frightened. He held the door wide open.

"Nina, come on. Let's get out of here," Eddie said.

The man in the green uniform turned around and looked at Eddie with a smirk on his face. I walked the perimeter of the bathroom to get as far away as possible from this man. I made it to the door and got to Eddie. Eddie was furious and kept his eyes on the strange man. The man stood there, staring Eddie down, as if saying *what are you going to do about it.*

"Lets go!" Eddie said.

Eddie and I hurried out of the bathroom.

"Where were you?" I asked. "You were supposed to be there waiting for me."

"I'm sorry, Nina," Eddie said. "The secretary from the office saw me and asked me to come into the office. She probably thought I was doing something wrong."

"I'm going home now," I said.

I left Eddie on the steps of the school and walked home alone as quickly as possible.

I confided in my mother that night and told her about my encounter with the man in the green uniform. I admitted that I was scared of him.

"¿Como se llama?" Mami asked.

"I don't know, Mami. I'll try to find out tomorrow when I

go back to work," I said.

"Okay Nina, let me know!" Mami said. "Be careful!"

~

I got up the next morning and went to work. I ran into the school's main office and reported my bathroom experience to the school's principal. Eddie was also there and he supported my story. The principal thanked me for reporting the strange man and told me that he would take care of it. He assured me that I would never have that same experience again.

Around eleven o'clock that morning, my father stopped by the school. I was surprised to see him there.

"Your mother told me what happened. I want to know who that pendejo is!" Papi said.

I could see the look in my father's eyes. He was angry and was already shaking his fists.

"Papi, I already took care of it. I reported him to the principal," I said. "He won't do it again. They're gonna fire him."

"Are you sure?" Papi asked.

"Si, Papi. I'm sure," I said. "That's what the principal said."

"Okay, but if he ever comes near you again, you better let me know!" Papi said.

"Okay, Papi," I said.

I gave my father a hug and watched as he climbed into his car. A sense of relief came over me. I never saw my father so angry and the last thing I ever wanted was to see him fight.

~

The summer went by fast. I enjoyed working, but what I liked most were my paychecks. My parents allowed me to spend my money on clothes and shoes for school. I felt all grown up. Eddie and I became good friends. As for the man in the green uniform, I never saw him again after that scary day in the bathroom, even after starting eighth grade at the same school.

When I went back to work the following summer, I was no longer afraid to enter the school. If I needed to use the bathroom, I had to go in the office to get a key. I liked that added security. It was nice that the office staff knew me. Therefore, they kept an eye on me each time I went in to use the bathroom.

31

New Friends. 1975.

During the summer of 1975, we moved to a bigger apartment in uptown Hoboken. It was summer time again. I was fifteen and I had just completed ninth grade. My newfound best friend was a girl name Cristina. She was two years younger than I was. At thirteen, Cristina was mature for her age, friendly, and very talkative. Out of all places, Cristina and I met in the laundromat on Cristina's block on 14th Street.

The washing machine in my new apartment had broken down and we were waiting for Papi to find time to fix it. I had never been in a laundromat before, but I assured my mother that I was capable of doing laundry.

"Hi. I've never seen you around here before. What's your name?" Cristina asked.

"My name is Nina," I responded as I struggled to put my clothes in the washing machine.

"I'm Cristina. I live upstairs. I come here all the time to do laundry for my mother," she said.

Cristina had already begun to wash her clothes.

"Is this your first time in a laundromat?" Cristina asked.

"Yes," I confessed. Cristina smiled.

"Look," she said, showing me what to do. "You open this flap and put the detergent here. You put the Downy there and then close the flap. Then you put your coins here." She took my coins and put them in the machine. "See how easy it is?" She was in a teaching mode.

The machine started to wash my clothes. Cristina truly impressed me.

Cristina was tall and slender, with long arms and hands that moved constantly and softly as she expressed herself in conversations. Her short, dark, wavy hair framed her light brown, narrow face. She had thin eyebrows and long eyelashes that made her deep-set, dark brown eyes stand out.

Cristina and I became inseparable. We met each other's parents and hung out in our apartments. We listened to music and tried to learn all of the new dance moves. We shared secrets and argued a lot. We were both brutally honest with each other. We held nothing back.

"I don't like your hair today. It looks messy," Cristina said.

"Well, I do!" I said.

"Your pants look too tight," I said.

"So?" Cristina said.

Several weeks after our friendship developed, we met two sisters who had just moved into an apartment on the same block where I lived. Nadine and Lucy were around the same age as Cristina and me. They didn't really look like sisters. At fifteen, Nadine was my height and weight with short dark wavy hair, brown eyes and thick glasses. Her light complexion, small pudgy nose, and dimples made her look very pretty. Lucy was fourteen years old and a little shorter and heavier than me. She had beautiful, long dark hair and brown eyes, pale creamy skin, and a fine straight nose. She was always smiling. Nadine and Lucy were nice and fun to be around. Cristina and I enjoyed hanging out with them.

One of our favorite hangouts was a candy store across the street from Cristina's apartment building. The candy store had boxes of candy surrounding the counter. Its three-tiered counter accommodated an assortment of treats. You could smell the sweetness of chocolate and bubble gum, the mintiness of peppermint candy, and the spiciness of Hot Tamales. On the wall to the left of the store hung racks of magazines and comic books. There were piles of newspapers on the floor. To the right of the store, next to the counter, was a glass soda refrigerator and next to it were two pinball machines that we enjoyed playing.

We hung out at the candy store every evening after school and during the summer months, just playing pinball. Cristina and I were very competitive with each other. Although we each had our own coins to play, we liked to play against each other using the two-player option.

Most of the time Cristina inserted the coin into the slot first so that she could start the game. She was very careful when she played. She kept her fingers on the flippers at all times and was very good at keeping the ball up in the game, earning lots of points with just one ball.

I was just as good. I would tilt the machine to finagle the ball into going where I wanted it to go. I was also good at trapping the ball. I would hold the ball in place with the flipper and shoot it where I wanted it to go.

"I got this," I said as I bumped the machine to get more points.

"You got nothing; I have more points than you!" Cristina said, moving her flippers as fast as she could.

"Match game! Yeah!" I screamed, holding my arms in the air.

"You cheat," Cristina said.

Lucy and Nadine rolled their eyes as they watched me and Cristina play. They didn't care so much for pinball. They just liked being around us. We enjoyed each other's presence.

Our families grew close, too. My parents enjoyed my friends. Whenever my parents planned our trips to the beach or to Tomahawk Lake, they insisted that I invite the girls.

"Did you invite the girls, Nina?" Mami would ask.

"Yes, Mami, and they're coming with us," I'd answer.

At Tomahawk Lake, we would walk around in our bikinis and take pictures as we tried to strike sexy poses. We enjoyed ordering virgin piña coladas and daiquiris. We pretended we were drunk as we sat by the bar of the outdoor beer garden. When we went into the water, we made sure we went in at waist-level just to avoid wetting our hair. Most of the time we preferred to ride the paddleboats over swimming.

32

Back to School.
September 1975.

September came around and we were back in school. Nadine and I were beginning our first year as sophomores at Hoboken High School. *Wow! Tenth grade,* I thought. Cristina and Lucy attended a junior high school that was near the high school. Going back to school was always very exciting for us. The girls and I liked getting all dressed up for school. Cristina, Nadine, Lucy, and I called each other every night to coordinate our outfits for the next school day.

"What are you wearing tomorrow?" Cristina asked.

"Jeans and my yellow blouse with wide sleeves," I answered.

Every morning we waited for each other at the corner of Fourteen and Bloomfield Street to walk to school together. We were typical teenage girls, talking about clothes, hair, and nails. We thought we looked like models dressed in long, flowing ruffled-sleeve tops and flared, tight jeans that covered our high-heeled shoes. With her tall physique, Cristina looked more like a sixteen-year-old than a thirteen-year-old. Even though she was taller and looked up to me because I was the oldest, Cristina had a mind of her own.

"Let's play pinball after school today," Cristina said.

"Yeah!" Lucy and Nadine said at the same time.

"No, I have to study. I'll play with you girls on Saturday," I said.

I took school more seriously than the other three girls did. I loved my friends, but I knew that Cristina, Lucy, and Nadine were not very interested in school and they all struggled in their classes.

I wanted to fulfill my lifelong dream of becoming a doctor. I knew that I had to study hard and get good grades in order to make my dream come true. Therefore, I came up with a routine. Every day after school, I went home, grabbed a glass of milk, and went to my room. I sat on my bed and surrounded myself with textbooks. I held one textbook on my lap, read a few pages, and took notes as I read. Writing helped me to retain information better.

The girls complained about their teachers all the time. Some of the teachers at our schools cared about their students. They came to class prepared to teach and really got into their lessons. Those were the good teachers. But a few teachers were cold and uncaring and didn't teach very well. They gave out assignments for the students to complete and expected them to complete the assignments without an introduction or a lesson. These teachers actually blamed the kids for not doing well. I was smart enough to realize that. So when I went home after school, I read my textbooks and practically taught myself what the teachers should have taught me. It worked, too. I did well on all of my tests.

Some evenings I would go over to Lucy and Nadine's apartment to help them with homework. When they were focused they understood the information, but when they were not, they just didn't get it. They were so into their novelas, too. Watching Spanish soap operas was their number one priority every evening. They would sit around with their mother and just watch one novela after another.

"Why do you watch novelas so much?" I would ask, frustrated.

"Because there's a love story in all of them," Nadine would say.

"The guys are cute," Lucy would say.

"But you guys have homework to do!" I said.

"The teachers don't care about us," Nadine said. "They just give us papers to work on and then they collect them. I'll do mine during homeroom period tomorrow."

"All right, I give up. Call me if you need help," I'd say.

I wasn't going to be sucked into those soap operas. To me they were a waste of time. I prefered to go back home and study all night. My mother was also a fan of soap operas, but she loved to see me study and so did my father. Papi would walk by my room just to see me with my books. He'd give me a kiss on my forehead and say, "Mi doctora." I knew that I was making him proud.

33

The Neighbor

The temperature was getting colder in November and the girls and I were now staying inside more often. Lucy, Nadine, and I each had our own things to do once we got home from school. I would wash a few dishes and then go to my room to study. Lucy would cook while her mother worked and Nadine would clean the house. Cristina, on the other hand, had her own plans.

Cristina, the social butterfly, was in the habit of visiting her neighbor, Connie, who lived down the hall from her. A short, heavy-set Hispanic woman with two kids, Connie looked like she was in her thirties. She was very friendly. One evening Cristina walked over to Connie's apartment and knocked on her door. Connie's son opened the door.

"Mami, it's Cristina!" He screamed.

"Hello, Ivan. How are you?" Cristina said. Ivan ran back to the living room where he had been watching TV. He didn't even say a word to Cristina.

"Hola, Cristina. Come in," Connie said.

"Hola, Connie," Cristina said. "What are you up to?"

"Oh, nothing. Just sitting here talking to my cousin," Connie said.

Cristina noticed a man sitting at Connie's dining room table. He smiled right away when he saw Cristina.

"This is my cousin, Pedro," Connie said. "He came from Puerto Rico."

Pedro stood up to greet Cristina. His eyes lit up when he saw her. He walked over to shake her hand. Cristina smiled and her eyes twinkled. She immediately noticed his short, stocky build. He was shorter than she, but his afro gave the illusion that he was taller. Pedro's nice smile, light skin, and small pointy nose caught Cristina's eye. *Handsome,* she thought.

"Me llamo Pedro," he said as he shook Cristina's hand. Cristina smiled.

"Me llamo Cristina," Cristina said. *Wow!* she thought. *He is even more handsome up close.*

Pedro only spoke Spanish, but that didn't stop their conversation. Cristina was also fluent in Spanish and they talked the entire afternoon. Connie looked at them and knew that they were instantly attracted to each other. She left them alone in the kitchen while she cared for her two young children.

Through her conversation with Pedro, Cristina learned that he was twenty years old.

"Twenty?" Cristina asked.

"Si. Is there anything wrong with that?" he asked.

Cristina looked at Pedro and then put her head down. She was trying to think. She didn't know if she should tell him her age.

"¿Que pasa?" he asked.

"Well... I'm only thirteen years old," Cristina said.

"Wow, you look older and you act older too!" he said.

"Yeah I know. Everyone tells me that," Cristina said.

"Age is only a number anyway," Pedro said. Cristina smiled.

~

The next morning, the girls and I met at the corner and walked to school together. Cristina couldn't resist. She couldn't wait to tell us about Pedro and how handsome he was. She gave us every detail about their conversation at Connie's house. She had a glow about her.

"Nina, guys, I have something to tell you," Cristina said.

"What?" I asked.

"I met a guy yesterday. He is so cute. His name is Pedro," Cristina said.

"How did you meet him?" I asked.

"Yeah, how?" Nadine asked.

"I met him yesterday when I went to Connie's house. He's her cousin," Cristina said. "I'm going to see him tonight. He's coming to the candy store to hang out with us. I want you girls to meet him. He may even bring his friends."

"What time?" Nadine asked.

"Around six o'clock," Cristina said.

"I'll be there," Lucy said.

"I don't know. I have to study tonight," I said. "I might or might not be there."

I decided to tag along and meet Pedro. Cristina seemed to have a crush on him. Since I was the oldest of the group, I felt it was my duty to see who he was. The girls and I met in the candy store that evening. We were playing a game of pinball when Pedro and his friends showed up. The guys smiled as they walked into the store. Cristina began the introduction.

"Lucy, Nadine, and Nina, this is Pedro," Cristina said.

"Hi," we all said.

"Hola," the guys said.

Judging by their accents, I could tell that they spoke mostly Spanish. Cristina had warned us that they might be like Pedro.

"Don't be surprised if his friends only speak Spanish, too," she said.

Pedro introduced the boys to the girls. One of Pedro's friends immediately took an interest in me. His name was Efrain and he spoke with a very thick accent. I thought he was cute—not gorgeous, just cute. He had freckles and curly hair. He was slender and taller than me by a couple of inches. Efrain came across as timid at first, but by the end of the night he was talking like there was no tomorrow. He talked about his life in Puerto Rico and his struggles there. He spoke like he had lived a lifetime. He talked about his happy and painful moments in Puerto Rico. He seemed very mature for being nineteen years old.

"I love Puerto Rico," Efrain said in a thick accent as he placed his right hand on his chest.

"So then, why did you move here?" I asked.

"I came here to find work," Efrain said. "Not too many jobs in PR. I was working on a farm picking mangoes and other fruit."

"Were you married?" I asked. I just had a gut feeling that he wasn't really single.

"Why do you ask that?" Efrain asked with a slight smile. He looked into my eyes. "No. I did live with a woman who had a kid, but it didn't work out."

"Why?" I asked as I took a step back.

"Sometimes things just don't work out," he said with a blank look on his face. He took a step toward me and looked into my eyes. "I believe that the right person is out there for me. What do you think?" He walked up to me and gently stroked my hair.

"Don't know what to say," I said as I looked down. The closer he got to me, the more nervous I got. There was something so appealing about him.

As I looked around the store, I could see Cristina playing pinball with Pedro. Lucy was in one corner talking to Pedro's brother, Papo. Papo was much taller than Pedro. He had straight hair and light-colored eyes. He looked older than Pedro, too. I couldn't believe they were brothers. He laughed a lot and kidded around with Lucy. I could see Lucy blushing. Ruben looked like his brother Efrain. He was a little taller and not shy at all. He was more like a comedian. He made Nadine laugh.

It was almost eight when I looked up at the clock. I moved away from Efrain and told each of the girls that we had to go home. Lucy and Nadine nodded and said goodbye to the guys. Cristina gave me a dirty look.

"I'm leaving soon," Cristina told me. I knew exactly what she meant by that. She wasn't ready to leave yet.

"You're going to get in trouble," I said.

"So?" she responded. I gave her a look that said *I can't believe you.*

I looked at Efrain and told him I had to leave.

"I have to go now," I said.

"When can I see you again?" he asked.

"I don't know," I said as I walked away.

I really didn't know when I would see Efrain again. All I wanted to do at that moment was go home to avoid any problems with my parents. Lucy, Nadine, and I walked out of the candy store together and went home. I was a little worried about Cristina. She stayed in the store with Pedro and his friends.

~

When I saw Cristina the next morning, she looked very happy. She said that she left the store shortly after we did and that Pedro had walked her home. She admitted to kissing him that night.

"The kiss felt so good," Cristina said. "I can't wait to see him again."

I could tell that Cristina was hooked on Pedro. By the look on Lucy and Nadine's faces, I could tell that they really liked Papo and Ruben as well. As for me, I would be lying if I said that I didn't think about Efrain that night. He was sweet and polite and I liked that about him.

At first we started seeing the guys during the weekends in a nearby park. Our parents didn't know that we were seeing them. We made sure we completed our chores at home and I made sure that I completed my homework before going anywhere. We would tell our parents that we were going out for a walk or to the park. Sometimes we would meet the guys at Connie's house. Enjoying the company, Connie was happy to have all of us over. The more and more we saw Connie, the closer she felt to us. She was like a big sister. We talked to her about the guys and she listened.

"Be careful," she once said. "Use protection. Don't get pregnant."

"We're not doing anything," I said.

"Just in case," Connie said.

Efrain began to come around the school more often to pick me up. We would walk home together. Out of the four guys, Efrain was the only one who didn't have a job. The other guys worked odd jobs. Efrain told me he was looking for work.

"I'm going to apply for a job tomorrow," Efrain said.

"Where?" I asked.

"At this shipping and receiving factory I saw in Union City yesterday," he said. "When I get the job, I'm going to take you to a lot of nice places," he promised.

I didn't answer him right away. I always thought that actions spoke louder than words.

"Let's see," I finally said.

34

Good Instincts

It was a warm day in February and Efrain and I were walk-ing through the park on my way home from school. He still didn't have a job. Efrain asked me to sit down on a bench. He said he wanted to talk for a few minutes. He took a deep look into my eyes and smiled. He said that he was very interested in me.

"You know wha'?" Efrain said in broken English. "I like you a lot."

"I like you too!" I responded as I tried to crack a smile.

He went to kiss my lips, but I quickly turned my head. I wasn't ready. I wanted to get to know him better.

"¿Que pasa?" He asked.

"I'm not easy. I want to wait a little longer," I said.

He blushed and looked at me as if I'd let him down. I heard a sigh and after a couple of seconds, he nodded.

"Okay," he said.

There was silence for a few minutes. He looked like a sad puppy dog. I started to feel sorry for him, but my gut feelings told me not to give in.

"I need to go home now," I said.

"Okay, I'll walk you to the next corner," he said.

We got off the bench and started walking again. We did not speak, not one word. When I got to the corner of 14th Street, I turned around and looked into his eyes.

"Gracias. Thank you for walking me home," I said.

I could see the sadness in his eyes. I started to feel sorry for him once again. I walked up to him and gave him a kiss on his cheek. He frowned and lowered his head. I took a step back, turned around, and walked away from him.

"I'll see you tomorrow." He smiled and slowly began to walk away.

~

I saw Cristina later in the evening. We were sitting outside on the steps of my apartment building. Cristina told me how she, Lucy, and Nadine had played hooky in the afternoon. She said that they went over to the guys' furnished apartments on Washington Street and spent the afternoon there.

"They live right on Third and Washington Street," Cristina said. "Ruben and Efrain share an apartment and Papo and Pedro share another apartment."

"What did you do over there?" I asked.

"We just hung out," Cristina said with a gigantic smile. "The guys had beer... and stuff."

"What stuff?" I asked.

"They smoked a joint," Cristina said.

"You didn't smoke, did you?" I asked.

"No. I just had a sip of their beer, that's all," Cristina said. "Efrain wasn't there."

"Yea, I know; he walked me home," I said. "I kind of feel sorry for him. He tried to kiss me but I wouldn't let him."

"Why?" Cristina said.

"I was afraid. He probably wanted something more than a kiss," I said. "I don't know. Something doesn't feel right."

"I know you like him. You should let him kiss you. He seems so shy," Cristina said.

"I know," I said.

Lucy and Nadine were walking up the street when they saw Cristina and me sitting around talking. They had big smiles and looked very happy.

"Did Cristina tell you what we did?" Lucy asked.

"Yeah, I heard," I said with a disappointed look on my face.

"Let's go take a walk down Washington Street," Nadine said. "Maybe we'll see the guys."

"Yeah! That's a good idea. Nina, we'll show you where they live," Cristina said.

By now, all eyes were on me. I could tell that all three girls wanted to take that walk. I was a little curious myself as to where the guys lived.

"Okay, let's go," I said.

We got up and off we went. We crossed Bloomfield Street, walked a block, and reached the corner of Fourteenth and

Washington Streets.

Washington Street was one of the main streets in Hoboken. The fourteen-block strip had just about everything. Most of the shopping centers and restaurants were located on downtown Washington Street, which was where the guys lived. The girls and I kidded around about what we would do if we saw the guys outside.

"I'm going to kiss him," Cristina said.

"Me too!" Nadine said. "Come on, Nina, give Efrain a kiss."

"Maybe," I said.

We got to the corner of Third and Washington Street and there was no sign of the guys outside. I looked up at the building and noticed someone looking out the window. It looked like a man dressed as a woman. I could see the Adam's apple on his neck. He had a square jaw and I noticed that he had patches of hair growing on the sides of his face. It almost looked like he had just shaved. He looked like he was wearing a blonde wig. What blew me away was that he had breasts and they looked real under his low-cut dress.

"Hi girls," he said in a high-pitched female voice when we walked by.

We all looked up. Cristina waved and said hello.

"Who's that?" I asked.

"That's Carla, el pato," she said.

"He's gay? I thought he was just a man dressed as a woman," I said.

"Didn't you see the boobs?" Cristina said.

"Ye—ah," I responded.

"Well they are real. He turned himself into a woman," Cristina said.

"How do you know him?" I asked.

"I met *her* today when I played hooky. She was in the hallway when I went to Pedro's apartment. Pedro introduced me to her," Cristina said.

"Carla?" I asked.

"Yeah, she went from Carlos to Carla," she said.

"Wow," I said.

We kept on walking down Washington Street. We looked at stores and pretended we were shopping. We made it all the way to First Street when we decided to turn around. On our way up Washington Street, we sat on the bench in front of City Hall. We were trying to figure out what to do next.

"Let's just go see them," Nadine said. "We should go up and knock on their door."

"Yeah, let's see what they're up to?" Lucy said.

Cristina and I looked at each other. "Okay," we both said.

We started walking again. As we slowly approached the building, I looked up to the second floor window to see if Carla was still there. *Nope, no sign of her,* I thought. We reached the entrance of the building. I hesitated to walk up the steps.

"Come on, girl. Let's get it over with," Nadine said.

"All right, I'm coming," I said.

I took a deep breath and up the steps I went. The girls made me lead. As we quietly walked up the stairs, I heard a commotion in the hallway. Someone was whispering up there, but I couldn't tell who it was. All of a sudden, I got a bad feeling. When we got to the second floor landing, I could see clearly where the whispering was coming from. What I saw next shocked me. I couldn't believe my eyes.

The two lovebirds were standing there wrapped in each other's arms. They had their eyes closed and were making out like there was no tomorrow. I could hear them moaning. They seemed to be enjoying each other. Carla opened one eye and saw me standing there. She didn't care! She closed her eyes and kept kissing Efrain. He had no idea that I was standing right behind him. I felt sick to my stomach and quickly became enraged.

"Cabrón!" I screamed. "Cabrón! I never want to see you again!"

Efrain turned around in shock. He couldn't even speak. Devastated, I started to run down the stairs. Efrain took a step forward to come after me.

"Wait, Nina!" he yelled.

Cristina turned around and screamed at Efrain.

"You creep! How could you do that?" she yelled.

Carla grabbed Efrain's arm and pulled him back.

"That's right! You girls can just get out of here," Carla said. "He's all mine."

I wanted to turn around and say something to him, or her, or whatever it was, but Cristina held me back.

"Let her go, Nina. She's not worth it and Efrain's not worth it!" Cristina said.

Outside, I turned and walked up Washington Street as I fast as I could. The girls followed close behind me.

"Wait, Nina," Nadine pleaded.

I spun around and gave her a dirty look.

"You knew, didn't you?" I said.

"What? I didn't know anything," Nadine said. "I swear!"

I looked at Cristina and took a deep breath.

"You knew that Efrain was screwing Carla, didn't you?" I asked.

"No way!" Cristina said. "It was just a coincidence that we caught him with her."

I walked home as fast as I could. The girls were having a hard time catching up to me. I didn't want to talk to anyone. As soon as I reached my apartment building I went right inside without saying a word to my friends. I ran up to my room and cried the entire night. I couldn't believe that I had fallen for Efrain. As I lay there in bed, I thought about what my mother once told one of her sisters:

"The quiet ones are the ones you have to watch."

"Mami, you were right," I whispered.

~

Efrain came around the school the next day. He waited for me to come out. The girls were waiting for me too.

"She doesn't want to talk to you," Cristina said.

"Come on, Nina," he said. "Let me talk to you."

I shook my head and kept walking. I couldn't even look at him. I was very angry with him but also disappointed in myself. I went home and cried.

"There's no way I'm ever going to let him get near me," I said to myself. "No way. No how."

Later in the evening, the girls came over to see me. They knew that I was sad and still upset.

"I'm sorry that he hurt you that way," Cristina said.

"That's okay. You didn't know," I said.

"I have something to tell you," Nadine said.

"What?" I asked.

"Ruben told me that Efrain sells pot. That's how he makes money," Nadine said.

"Why didn't you tell me?" I asked.

"I just found out today," Nadine said. "That's why I came over here."

"Yeah, Nina. Don't be mad at us; we didn't do anything. We didn't know," Lucy said.

The fact that Efrain was a drug dealer turned me off even more. I didn't want to see him ever again. The girls tried to make me laugh by making fun of Efrain and Carla.

"Boy, he must have been desperate," Cristina said.

"Yeah, she or he is nothing compared to you Nina," Nadine said.

"You were too good for him," Lucy said.

They finally had me smiling. After a few more compliments

I was laughing and having fun with the girls all over again.

"Hey, Nina, I have a new record that I want you to listen to," Cristina said.

"What's it called?" I asked.

Cristina took a vinyl record out of her bag. The group on the cover was called Los Terricolas. She played the LP on my portable record player.

"This is the song that I like. It's called "Una Carta," Cristina said.

The ballad was beautiful and sentimental. The singer sang the song with all of his heart. He was asking his girlfriend for forgiveness. I was drawn to his voice. The melody warmed my heart. After the second verse, I started to cry. The song reminded me of Efrain.

The girls hugged me. Cristina stopped the record player.

"Nina, what's wrong?" The girls asked at the same time.

"What do you think?" I said. "The song reminds me of Efrain. I'm so stupid!"

"Sorry Nina. We didn't mean to make you cry. I just wanted you to hear it," Cristina said.

"That's all right. I do like the song. I just have to get over Efrain—that's all," I said.

"Well, Lucy and I have to go now," Nadine said. "By the way, we're not going to school tomorrow. We have to go with mom to the Bronx to visit our sick uncle, so don't wait for us at the corner tomorrow morning."

"Okay," I said.

"I'm leaving too," Cristina said. "See you in the morning, Nina."

"See you tomorrow, Cristina," I said.

The girls had already left when I noticed that the record was still on the record player. "Sh—!" I said under my breath. I got up from my bed and went to take a shower. The hot shower felt good. It soothed my aching muscles and heart. After the shower, I was ready to go to bed. I walked by the living room where my parents were watching TV and asked them for their blessings, a religious custom that Puerto Rican children learn at a young age. To me it was more than religious; it was a way of showing love and respect.

"Bendición, Mami," I said.

"Dios te bendiga," Mami said.

"Bendición, Papi" I said.

"Dios te bendiga," Papi said.

I went to bed, but couldn't resist listening to that song one more time. I turned on the record player, lowered the volume and played the LP. I couldn't get that voice out of my head. I listened to every word in that song. Wow, I thought. As soon as the song was over, I turned my record player off. I couldn't stop thinking about the day I met Efrain. He was sweet and gentle. And now he was a totally different person. *What a fool I was.*

35

Terror

The next morning, I got up to go to school when my phone rang. It was Cristina saying that she was not going to school. She said she was sick and that her mother told her she could stay home.

"Okay," I said. "I'll stop by after school to see you."

Now I have to walk to school by myself, I thought. I got dressed and out the door I went. Although the last few days had been unusually warm, it was once again starting to feel like February should: cold and dry. I went back inside to get my brand new brown corduroy jacket. I couldn't wait to wear it. I buttoned it up to stay warm. I looked at the corner where I normally met the girls and no one was around. It felt weird walking to school alone.

I made it to school on time, went to all of my classes, and did all of my work. When the bell rang at three o'clock I packed up some of my books that I needed for homework and put them in my book bag. My notebook couldn't fit into my bag, so I carried it in my hands and walked out of the classroom. I looked around the halls in search of Nadine, but then I remembered her telling me that she and Lucy were not coming to school today either. I left the school and walked up Clinton Street.

Homework was on my mind. I was trying to figure out which assignment to do first once I got home. All of a sudden, I felt someone behind me. When I turned around, I came face to face with him. It was Efrain.

He looked different. His eyes were red and he reeked of alcohol. His serious facial expression scared me. He was wearing a long black trench coat that I had never seen before. He grabbed my right arm and held me close to his body. I felt something hard in his coat pocket.

"What are you doing?" I said.

"You are coming with me!" he said, squeezing my arm.

"Where are you taking me?" I asked.

I felt my stomach turning. My hands started to shake. I tried to break free but he held my arm tighter. I was ready to scream when he covered my mouth with his other hand. He pressed his right hip against my left hip. He wanted to make sure that I felt whatever he was carrying in his pocket.

"Walk and don't scream!" he said. "I don't want to hurt you."

"Don't hurt me; please don't hurt me," I said.

I looked in his eyes and all I could see was evil. He looked like a devil to me and it scared me to death. I could feel my heart racing. I kept my eyes on him as I wondered where he was taking me. When I looked straight ahead on Clinton

Street, I knew exactly where we were going.

I could see the Viaduct on 14th Street clearly from Ninth and Clinton Street. The 14th Street Viaduct connected Hoboken, Union City, and Jersey City Heights. It was always busy and noisy. Even if I screamed there, no one would probably hear me. He was taking me under the bridge. The place was isolated; there was nothing there but trusses and steel holding the bridge up.

Students were walking home from school. Most of them were used to seeing the two of us together, especially since Efrain always walked me home from school.

"Hello," the students said to Efrain and me as they walked by us.

Efrain smiled back. "Hola," he said as he squeezed my arm tightly. He gave me a look that said, *you'd better keep your mouth shut.*

All kinds of thoughts were flying through my head now. *How could I have been so stupid? What did I do that would make him want to hurt me?*

We walked all the way up to 14th Street. Instead of turning right to walk toward my apartment building, we continued straight ahead to the underpass. We were now under the bridge and only a couple of blocks away from my home. I was terrified.

"What the hell? Why are you bringing me here?" I asked. "Efrain, please let me go."

"You're not going anywhere!" he said.

Efrain spun me around to face him and threw my notebook and book bag on the ground. He wrapped his arms around my waist and tried to kiss my lips. I kept moving my head. *No way is he going to kiss me*, I thought. I pulled away from him and managed to get loose, but he reached out and pulled me by my hair. Then he grabbed my waist and started spinning me around. I flailed my arms and legs to try to escape, but he only held me tighter. I started to feel dizzy.

Efrain laughed. "You're mine now," he said.

He threw me on the ground and climbed on top of me. I began to scream. He punched me in the face so hard I could see stars before my eyes. Tears poured down my face. I felt paralyzed as he straddled me. By now, he was panting. He ripped the buttons off my brand new corduroy jacket.

"Don't Efrain, please." I pleaded, begging him to let me go.

I knew I had to fight back, but the weight of his body was crushing me like a huge rock. I closed my eyes for a second and said a quick prayer to God. *Please God, save me. Don't let him take away what I have protected for so long.* Staying a virgin until I got married meant a lot to me. It was something that was instilled in me after hearing a priest give a lecture one day on sexual relations between a man and a woman. He stressed how pre-marital sex is against Catholic teachings and that sexual relations complete a marriage. I wanted to save myself for the man that I would marry, and I didn't want anyone taking that away from me.

I screamed as loud as I could and this time he punched

me on the other side of my face even harder. I lost consciousness for a moment. Efrain panicked and started to shake my
shoulders. I guess he wanted to make sure that I was still alive.
I tried to open my eyes but only managed to open the right
one. My left eye was badly swollen. Looking up with my right
eye, I realized that my biggest nightmare wasn't over. Efrain
was smiling over me.

As I lay there, practically lifeless, I felt him loosening my
blouse like a savage beast from the jungle. There was nothing
I could do. I felt trapped under his body. I found myself in
another state of mind. I started dreaming about my parents. In
my head I could hear Mami crying and feel Papi's devastation,
both grief-stricken and heartbroken over my ordeal. *A father's
worst nightmare*, I thought.

Suddenly, a loud noise snapped me back to reality. A
miracle had occurred. I heard the sound of a vehicle close by.
The driver was blowing his horn at Efrain. I could see flashes
of a siren. The sound stopped Efrain in his tracks. He looked at
the driver, jumped to his feet, and ran. I could hear the sound
of a CB radio. A man was calling 911.

"Are you all right?" he asked.

"I'm okay," I nodded. My head was pounding and my left
eye was swollen shut.

"I'm getting you help," he said.

Within minutes there were police officers everywhere. I
could hear the siren of an ambulance. The attendants came
running towards me.

"Can you hear me?" the attendant asked.

I tried nodding my head, but didn't have any strength left.

"What's your name?" he asked.

I tried very hard to say my name. I took in a deep breath.

"Ni-na, Ni-na Tava-rez," I said.

"She's got a pulse!" an attendant said.

"Blood pressure is ninety over sixty," reported the other attendant.

One of the attendants tried to look into my eyes with a flashlight. He looked in my right eye without any problems. My left eye was a different story, but he managed to open it slightly.

"Oh my God, her eye is swollen shut. Too much edema," the attendant called out. "Let's take her to the hospital."

The attendants put some kind of brace around my neck, lifted me off the ground and onto a stretcher, then carried me into the ambulance.

"Where are you taking her?" the police officer asked.

"We are taking her to the medical center in Jersey City," the one attendant replied. "She said her name is Nina Tavarez."

"Copy that," the police officer said.

As the attendant drove the ambulance, I fell into a deep sleep. I started dreaming about Mami and Papi again. I could hear them cry. *I'm so sorry, Mami and Papi. I didn't mean to hurt you. Please don't cry. I'll be all right, I promise.*

When we arrived at the emergency room, the ambulance attendants gently lifted my gurney and took me inside. We went through a huge glass door and into the emergency room. Once inside, the staff moved quickly. I could hear the ambulance attendant talking to one of the nurses. Although my eyes were closed, I could hear voices around me.

"Her name is Nina Tavarez. We found her under the Viaduct in Hoboken. She was slipping in and out of consciousness. Her vital signs are stable. She has a huge hematoma on the left eye. Pupils are equal and reactive to light. Possible rape victim," the attendant reported.

"All right," I heard the female nurse say.

That was the last thing I heard.

~

Several hours later, I woke up to the sound of Mami crying. I tried to open my eyes but my left eye was still swollen shut. I could feel a patch over it. I saw Papi sitting next to me holding my hand. Tears of joy filled my eyes and soon they were like a river streaming down my face. I was thankful to be alive, but most importantly I was happy to see my parents again.

"Pa-pi, Ma-mi," I tried to say.

"Don't talk now, Nina. You have to rest. We are here for you," Papi said.

"I'm sor-ry," I said.

"Sorry for what?" Mami asked as she took a deep breath.

"Sorry for causing you pain," I managed to let out.

"Nina, you don't have to be sorry for anything," Mami said

as she held my hand and kissed it.

"It's not your fault," Papi said as he tried to contain himself.

I looked around with my right eye; I could see Mami and Papi crying. They got up and reached over to hug me.

~

Several days went by and I was already on the road to recovery. The doctor said that I was in shock and had a concussion. I had minor bruises all over my body from being thrown on the ground. The doctor removed the patch from my left eye, which was still very bruised and swollen. He said that my left eye would take time to heal and that I would need frequent eye examinations to make sure that the blow to the eye did not affect my vision. The doctor suggested that I wear sunglasses all the time while in and out of school to avoid having people stare at it.

My parents stood by me and held my hand as I asked the doctor a very important question about that day under the Viaduct.

"Okay, doctor. How far did he get with me?" I asked.

The doctor looked at me. I could see my parents smiling.

"Not far Nina. You still had your pants on when you got to the hospital," he said.

"Really?" I asked.

"Yes, really. You are still a virgin," he said.

I took a deep breath and smiled. Mami and Papi hugged

me tight. It was such a beautiful moment. *Thank you, God,* I thought. *I am so blessed.*

36

The Days After

In the days after the terror, I thought about Efrain. I wondered how I could have been so stupid. The signs were there early on, but I was too naïve to see them. Let's see—he was nineteen years old, spoke like he had lived a lifetime, never told me what brought him to Hoboken from Puerto Rico, and was unemployed. He was also a high school dropout. Later into our relationship, I found him making out with a transsexual and discovered that he was dealing drugs. Obviously, he was not for me. I should have been smarter.

Efrain Tinoco got away and was never found. His brother Ruben also vanished. Their friends, Pedro and Papo, swore to the police that they had no idea where they were. I suspect that Efrain and Ruben flew back to Puerto Rico and went into hiding.

Cristina and Lucy continued to see Pedro and Papo despite my traumatic experience with Efrain. The girls swore that their boyfriends were different and not like Efrain. I agreed. To me, Pedro and Papo were hard workers and seemed to be very concerned about what happened to me. The girls met with the guys without their parents' knowledge, but only when they could. All eyes were on us now. The people in our neighborhood, including our parents, watched over us in a good way. They wanted to protect us so they started to question our every move.

Still best friends, Cristina, Nadine, Lucy, and I continued to walk to school together. After school, they came by my apartment every day to make sure that I was okay.

"Nina, do you need anything?" Cristina asked.

"No, I'm okay," I said.

"You want to go to the movies on Saturday?" Lucy asked.

"No, I really don't want to go out," I said.

"We're just trying to get your mind off things," Nadine said.

"I'm okay. A little scared, I think, but I'll be okay," I said.

I had no desire to go anywhere after school or on weekends. Instead I focused on my studies. Spring was coming and I enjoyed studying by the window. I could feel the warm sun streaming through my window. Trees were blooming and birds were flying everywhere. As I looked out the window, I thought about my future and my life-long dream. Nothing had really changed. I still had the same dream that I had when I was five years old. Becoming a doctor would be a reality for me someday. I was more excited now than ever. No one would ever take that dream away from me.

As time went by, I tried to forget *that day*, the most terrifying ordeal I had ever experienced. My emotional wounds, though, were here to stay. The scar above my left eye would also make it impossible for me to forget that terrifying day. I even blamed myself for what happened, but my family and friends reminded me often that it was never my fault. I also went to church as often as I could, especially when my fears and pain were just too unbearable. Faith seemed to always find a way into my heart to ease the pain.

I thought I would always have trust issues. I was learning to analyze people to see if they had good or bad intentions. I noticed body language, approaches, and ways of thinking. I also looked for hidden agendas. Although, I didn't really like this analytical side of me, it was becoming my very own body guard—a way to protect myself from any potential harm. Who could blame me?

37

Goals Accomplished

Two years had passed since my traumatic experience with Efrain and, at the age of eighteen, I was finally graduating from high school. There were plenty of smiles, a few tears, and many hugs at my high school graduation. Hundreds of people sat on the bleachers as the class of 1978 graduated. I looked over to Mami and Papi as I approached the stage to get my diploma. Their eyes were gleaming as they stood and clapped their hands. I saw Bobby holding his arms up in a V for victory. I could hear my friends Cristina and Lucy whistling and applauding. Nadine was sitting with the rest of the graduates; she had already gone up to get her diploma. After the ceremony, we all gathered in front of the stage to take pictures.

"I am so proud of you, hija," Papi said, hugging me.

"Um, mi hija," Mami said, stroking my hair and kissing my forehead.

Bobby walked over to me and said, "High five, sis!" He slapped his palm against mine.

I turned around to the sound of soft giggles and there they were, my girls, Cristina, Nadine, and Lucy. Cristina was now a sophomore at the high school and Lucy was a junior. Both were looking forward to their own graduations. Nadine and I congratulated and hugged each other tightly. Cristina and Lucy came over and we celebrated with a big team hug. We were so proud of each other.

Looking back, I remember how unbearable my last two years of high school were as I tried to comprehend Efrain's actions. Why did he hurt me that way? Graduating from high school meant that I had attained the knowledge I needed to prepare myself for bigger challenges that would take me to the next level in life. That's all. And now I was ready for college.

I remember receiving my acceptance letter from Rutgers University last fall for their pre-med program. I would be majoring in biology. I was so excited to receive the letter, especially since I had applied to other colleges, but Rutgers was my number one choice.

"Papi, Mami, I got in," I shouted after reading the acceptance letter. "I'm going to Rutgers. Yeah!"

"Dios te bendigas, hija," Mami said as she gave me a kiss on my cheek.

"Congratulations, Nina," Papi said. "I knew you could do it!"

My college graduation meant more to me than high school. It was an important milestone in my life, a culmination of all my hard work, uneventful and trauma-free. The chemistry and physics courses were challenging; I had to study hard. However, I managed to maintain a 4.0 GPA, which showed strong study habits and work ethics. Passing my Medical College Admission Test (MCAT) was such a blessing. This standardized test was part of the medical school admission process and one of the hardest tests that I have ever taken in my life.

As for graduating from medical school, well, what can I say? It was the beginning of my lifelong dream. Nina Tavarez was finally going to be a doctor. However, getting into medical school was very challenging. The competition for medical school admission was intense. Many candidates applied and only a few got in. I was one of the lucky ones.

Although the last two years of medical school involved more hands-on-patient work, I felt that it was much tougher than college in the sense that I had to study more in a shorter amount of time. On average, I was getting three to four hours of sleep per night. I wanted to do well so that I could get into a decent residency program upon graduating from medical school. There were times when I thought I wouldn't make it. I remember talking to my father about medical school on the phone one afternoon.

"Papi, it is so hard," I said.

"You can do it," Papi said. "I will say a prayer for you. God is with you and he will keep you strong."

That was all it took. Hearing my father's words and his vote of confidence kept me strong. No matter how hard things were, I was going to make it through and graduate from medical school.

Part Two

38

Becoming a Doctor

At twenty-six years of age I graduated from medical school and managed to enroll in a residency program at the medical center in Jersey City, the same hospital that treated me after my brutal attack. Residency training is a mandatory training which follows medical school. As a resident physician, I practiced medicine under the supervision of a fully licensed physician; an *attending* is what we residents called them. Although I practically lived in the hospital, I had come to realize that even after working ungodly hours for minimum pay, I loved my job. I enjoyed working with my patients, practicing medicine, and doing all the things you see doctors do on television.

I loved the challenges placed on me when I was grilled on issues related to my patients.

"Dr. Tavarez, what is your diagnosis of Mr. Williams?" Dr. George, the attending physician asked.

"Sir, I believe the patient is suffering from congestive heart failure," I answered.

"Based on what?" he asked

"Patient complains of dizziness, fatigue, weakness, and shortness of breath. Lungs auscultated for rales bilaterally. He's coughing up frothy sputum and has edema of the ankles and legs. He has a history of hypertension and X-ray shows enlarged heart with fluid buildup. Capillary refill is greater than three seconds. Cardiac enzymes are elevated," I said.

"Nice work, doctor," Dr. George said.

The bulk of my day was spent seeing patients in the emergency room, following up with them at the clinic, writing orders, changing dressings, completing procedures, reviewing test results, etc. And yes, it was stressful at times; however, I looked forward to completing my residency and working at this hospital as an ER doctor.

As for my personal life, well, it was practically nonexistent. I was on-call pretty much all the time and worked all kinds of shifts, leaving me no choice but to stay in the hospital overnight on a regular basis. If I was lucky, I would go to my new apartment on Hudson Street in Hoboken, sleep for a little while, then report back early for morning rounds. I saw Mami and Papi as much as I could. They moved out of their apartment on 14th Street and were now living in an apartment on Willow Avenue in Hoboken. Bobby had moved back to New York City to work for an architectural firm. He was a successful architect in Manhattan and lived in a nice studio apartment. Therefore, I only saw him at my parents' apartment during the holidays and on special occasions. I was very proud of my brother Bobby. Not only did he achieve his dream of becoming an architect, he managed to also buy his lifelong prized possession, a yellow corvette.

As for my friends, we saw each other from time to time. The guys, Pedro and Papo, were now a thing of the past. Cristina and Lucy had broken up with them a few months after my ordeal with Efrain. Cristina was now working as a therapist at a center for mental health and illness. She was still single and was taking courses to become a psychologist. Lucy became a social worker at a children's home and was happily married with three kids—one girl and two boys. Nadine worked as a pediatric registered nurse at the medical center where I worked. We ran into each other sometimes. A single mother, Nadine also had three kids—one girl and two boys. They all seemed to be quite busy with their personal lives.

39

Déjà Vu

Two years into my residency, I was now on call more than ever. It was three o'clock in the morning. I had just jumped into bed in one of the resident's quarters when I got the call to report to the emergency room. I had barely slept in the last two nights. The ER had been in full mode for several nights with all kinds of traumas. I rushed out of bed, put on my blue scrubs, and brushed my teeth.

Upon entering the trauma area, I heard a mother scream. The shrill sound of her voice sent chills up and down my spine. A short Hispanic woman standing outside a room waved me down as she cried desperately for help.

"Ay dios mio, please help my daughter!" she said.

"Hi, I'm Dr. Tavarez. What's going on?" I asked the woman as I entered the room.

"Please, my daughter, look!" she said as she bowed her head and folded her hands in front of her. "Somebody beat her. I found her in the hallway almost naked!"

I looked at the girl and my heart sank. She had bruising all over her face and arms. I noticed a deep cut on her head. Her right eye was swollen shut. *Boy, what a beating*, I thought.

I felt anxiety wash over me and I suddenly had a flashback. This was the same room that I was in twelve years ago. I tried to keep my cool. I picked up the patient's chart and read her name: Noelia Rodriguez.

"¿Señora Rodriguez?" I asked the mother.

"Si," she said.

"When did this happen? Did anyone call the police?" I asked. "How old is she?"

"Si, I called the police. He's over there. I found her around one this morning," the mother said. "She is fifteen years old."

"Was she conscious or unconscious, despierta, when you found her?" I asked.

"Awake, but she was falling in and out of sleep at the same time," the mother said.

I proceeded to assess the girl. On examination, the patient was lethargic but oriented to time and place. I didn't see any signs of brain or spinal injuries. She was moving both arms and legs. Her vital signs—pulse, respirations and blood pressure—were normal. Lungs were clear.

However, the closer I looked, the more nervous I became. Noelia had bruising on her abdomen and between her thighs. I noticed her dress, but no underwear. *Rape victim*, I thought. I stepped out of the room to ask a nurse for assistance.

"Dottie, could you help me here, please?" I asked. Dottie had experience working with rape victims in the ER. In fact, she was one of the best nurses that I had ever worked with.

"Possible rape victim," I whispered as I proceeded back into the room and grabbed the chart. I checked for parental consent before proceeding with my questions.

"Okay, doctor," Dottie said. She came into the room, gathered some supplies from the cabinets, and waited for my signal. Dottie brought a chair for the mother and asked her to sit by her daughter.

"What did you mean when you said that she was almost naked when you found her?" I asked the mother. "Did she have any clothes on?"

"This is how I found her, with this dress and no underwear," she said.

I could see the pain in Mrs. Rodriguez's eyes. Tears streamed down her face.

"Noelia, can you hear me?" I asked.

"Yes," she said, trying to move her swollen lower lip.

"Do you remember what happened?" I asked. I began documenting her responses.

"Yes," she said as she opened and closed her left eye. "I was at a party at my neighbor's upstairs. I knew that I had to leave by midnight to get ready for school the next day, so I said goodbye to everyone there and left. Somebody followed me down the stairs and grabbed me from behind. He covered my mouth." Noelia began to cry uncontrollably.

I pulled a chair over and sat next to her. Leaning over and stroking her hair, I provided reassurance.

"We are here to help you Noelia; you are safe now," I said

sympathetically. "Can you tell me what happened next?"

"He raped me. He said he would kill me if I screamed. I just closed my eyes and lay there," she said as she took a deep breath.

"Do you know who did this to you?" I asked.

"No, it was too dark and I kept my eyes closed. I was scared," she said. "Oh, wait, he had a thick accent. I think he was Spanish."

"Okay, you will be all right," I assured her as I held her hand. "Noelia, Dottie and I need to examine you."

"Okay," Noelia said.

"Señora Rodriguez, we need to put a gown on your daughter and do an internal exam. Are you okay with that? It's very important that we do this," I said.

The mother looked into my eyes. She held her shoulders back and in a steady, low-pitched voice she said, "Do what you have to. Just help my daughter."

I nodded. "I will," I assured her.

Dottie and I stood over a counter as we put on our gloves. We assisted Noelia in disrobing as she sat on the examination table; she was too weak to stand. Dottie cautiously contained any fallen debris and fibers on the examination table paper. We placed her dress in a bag. Prior to putting a gown on the patient, Dottie took pictures of her injuries. We obtained blood and urine specimens and swabs of the oral cavity. We then placed the patient in stirrups.

"Noelia, this is going to feel a little uncomfortable, but I have to do this," I said.

"Go ahead," she said. "It's okay."

I conducted an examination of her perineum and vagina. I collected the necessary specimens. Dottie made sure to seal and date all evidence. After the examination, we assisted the patient into a comfortable position and provided reassurance.

I walked up to Noelia and held her hand. "Noelia, I'm going to ask a social worker to come in to talk to you—one who specializes in these kinds of cases. A police officer will also be coming in to ask you questions. I'll be around here for another hour or two, but I promise to come back to check up on you."

"Okay," Noelia said.

I walked up to Noelia's mother and gave her a hug. "I'm ordering X-rays just to check for broken bones. Call me if you need anything," I said.

Dottie and I left the room. I made a few phone calls at the nurses' station and wrote some orders while Dottie handled the specimens. I saw the officer speaking to an ambulance attendant. I slowly walked up to him and introduced myself.

"Hi, I am Dr. Tavarez. I just finished examining Miss Rodriguez. You may go in now to ask her questions," I said.

"Well, hello. I'm Officer Lee, Larry Lee," he said as he looked into my eyes. "It's nice to meet you."

I shook my head and barely smiled. I was tired and looked like a mess. "She's ready now," I said as I walked away.

I left the ER and, as tired as I was, I proceeded to go the chapel to say a prayer for Noelia. The chapel offered staff, patients, and visitors a place for individual prayers and mediations. Located near the hospital's main lobby, the chapel was essentially a small meditation room. It had a few pews and kneelers. On the front wall of the chapel were two stained glass windows with a large crucifix fixed between them.

As a resident, I no longer had time to attend weekly mass. The chapel was now my place for worship and prayers for my patients and family—a place for me to pray during emotional times. Soon after I entered the chapel, I made the sign of the cross, walked up to the crucifix, kneeled, and folded my hands in front of me. I then began my prayer for Noelia.

"Please Lord, keep her safe..."

Afterward, I went back to my bed in the resident's quarter and slept for about an hour. By this time, it was five o'clock in the morning. I woke up an hour later, got myself together, and rushed back to the ER to see Noelia.

Noelia had a robe on and was ready to be discharged. I conferred with the social worker and then checked in with my attending. Noelia had no broken bones and was free to go home.

"Please make an appointment at the clinic for a followup," I said.

Noelia and her mother nodded and within a few minutes after receiving my discharge instructions, they left the ER.

I had seen many rape cases here in the hospital, but

Noelia's case got to me. It brought back bad memories. It made me think about that day under the Viaduct in Hoboken. Efrain was never caught. *Could he still be around?* I wondered.

40

The Recreation Center

I left the hospital at four p.m. for a quick change of clothing at my apartment. Kids of all ages were expecting me at the recreation center in Jersey City at six. I typically met with them there once a month to assist with homework or just to give them pep talks. Many of these kids lived in poverty and were currently being raised in the projects. They seemed to enjoy having me around. I remember what a little girl said to me the month before.

"I want to be a doctor just like you," she said, smiling with dreamy eyes.

"Oh no, honey. You're going to be better than me," I said as I gave her a hug.

The kids inspired me so much. They made me laugh and filled my heart with joy.

As I drove home from the hospital, I became preoccupied with Noelia. I couldn't get her out of my mind. She was a victim of a violent act. I asked myself the same question that I had asked twelve years ago: *why?* However, now I knew why.

Rape is about power and submission. Most rapes are

performed by men, though some men have been victims too. To the male rapist, it is a way to confirm his manhood. Rape from the victim's perspective is a brutal and terrifying act. The experience is extremely painful. It's like someone is ripping you apart. I needed to see Noelia again just to tell her this and to make sure she was all right. I knew that self-blame would soon kick in. And if she didn't have a good support system, Noelia would endure psychological problems.

I arrived at my apartment building on Hudson Street, parked my car in the front, and went upstairs to my apartment on the second floor. I opened the door—*Whew! What smells?* I thought. I walked over to my kitchen where the odor was coming from and there it was: week-old rotting garbage right in my kitchen trash can. I could see the chicken bones from the chicken that I ate several days ago. *Wow! I've been away that long?* After taking the lid off the can, I tied the ends of the plastic bag together and took it out of the can. I grabbed my keys and out the door I went to dispose of the stinky trash. Then I came back inside and sprayed the entire apartment with Lysol disinfectant, hoping to kill the odor.

Except for the odor in the kitchen, my one-bedroom apartment was pretty clean. My kitchen was small and narrow with updated cabinets. My living and dining area occupied the same room. The comfy brown sofas, round dining table, and light hardwood floors made the apartment look homey. My apartment lacked character; the plain white walls were just that. Because of my work schedule and little pay, I had no time or money to decorate.

With just a little over an hour to spare before leaving for the recreation center, I decided to do some dusting. Afterward, I took a quick shower, applied some makeup, and dressed in a T-shirt and pair of jeans. I grabbed my purse and proceeded to walk out of my apartment. I double-checked to make sure that my door was locked before I left.

The rush hour traffic from Hoboken to Jersey City was terrible. I should have known better; I should have left the apartment earlier. After arriving at the rec center late—six thirty, to be exact—I parked my car and ran up the steps.

The recreation center was in an old, tall, red-brick, three-story building. On the first level was an indoor basketball court with bleachers all around. Kids played basketball there all the time after school and during the summer. To the side of the court were small rooms. Two were restrooms, one was a storage room, and the other was a large room with a few computers. Kids normally came to this room to work on homework. The center tried to have an adult present at all times to supervise the kids and assist with homework. These kids were lucky if they had more than two adults on the same day.

Most of the time it was only Mr. Butler, the director, who supervised the kids as some played on the court and others studied in the computer room. Mr. Butler was a tall and slightly overweight African American man with gray hair and a nice smile. He reminded me of a sweet grandfather, but God forbid you stepped on his toes or made him angry. He would not hesitate to put you in your place. He ran a tight ship in the center.

"Pick up the balls and put them where they belong before you leave," Mr. Butler would say.

"Yes sir," the kids would respond.

Lack of staff was one of the reasons why I volunteered to come here once a month. These kids needed more than supervision; they needed a mentor and someone who could understand them. When I opened the door, I saw kids sitting on the bleachers waiting for me.

"She's here!" said a girl with sparkling eyes.

"Nina!" they shouted when they saw me. They jumped up and down and waved.

"Hi guys, how are you?" I asked as I smiled and hugged each one.

"I knew you would come," little Marilyn said as she hugged me. "You always do!"

Marilyn was a five-year-old Ecuadorian girl with long black hair and dark eyes. She had the most beautiful dark eyelashes. She seemed bright for her age and sometimes she sounded like an adult.

"My name is Marilyn Monrroy, almost like the famous actress," she once told me.

Little Matthew was also excited to see me. He was about eight years old and thin, with dirty blond hair, light skin, and green eyes. The top of his head came up to my shoulders. He grabbed my hand and guided me toward the bleachers.

"Sit Nina, please," Matthew said. "We want to hear the story."

"What story?" I asked.

"The story of how you became a doctor," little Johnny said. Ten years old with light brown skin and brown eyes, Johnny was such a cute little boy. They were all cute.

The kids asked many questions on how to become a doctor. I was happy to answer every one.

"I knew I wanted to become a doctor since I was five years old," I said. "Never give up on your dreams; anything is possible. You just have to really want it and study hard."

"Are there a lot of girl doctors?" Marilyn asked.

"Yes," I said. "And there will be many more in the future."

"Are there a lot like us?" Julie asked as she folded her hands in front of her. A curious child, she loved to read and enjoyed learning new things. At nine years old, she had long, dark, straight hair reaching all the way down to her waist. She had dark, almond-shaped eyes and a pretty smile.

"What do you mean?" I asked. I knew what she meant, but I wanted her to tell me.

"Well, Spanish, like us," Julie said.

I looked at all the kids as they sat around me. They were of many races. Some were Puerto Rican, a few were Colombian, several were African American, four were Caucasian, and two were Ecuadorian.

"Yes, there are a lot of doctors just like all of us!" I said. "Doctors come in every race and color, and speak different languages."

"Nina, I have show-and-tell in my school every month. Could you please, pretty please, come to my school?" Marilyn asked. "I want to show my friends and teachers that my friend is a doctor who speaks Spanish. Please?"

"Just let me know when and I'll try to be there," I said.

"Good, I'll find out for you," Marilyn said.

"I can't promise you anything because of my work at the hospital, but I will try to make it," I said.

It was eight o'clock in the evening and time to wrap things up. I gave each kid a hug before leaving the rec center.

"I'll be back next month," I said. "And Marilyn, let me know when you need me."

"Bye, Nina," they all said as they waved goodbye.

I got in my car and drove home. Immediately after entering the apartment, I locked the door and hooked the chain. I lived alone and needed to feel secure. Remembering that I had morning rounds to do at the hospital, I set my alarm for five o'clock in the morning. Then I hit the bed and tried to fall asleep.

~

After a few hours of sleep I jumped up, feeling a profound sense of fear. I was sweating and my heart was pounding in my ears. I began to pant hard as I looked around the room. It was a dream—no, it was a nightmare. But I couldn't remember it all. I just remembered seeing Tia Josephina and Efrain looking down at me and whispering to each other. I couldn't hear what they were saying, but it scared me to death and I had a hard time falling back asleep. I woke up at five a.m. and got ready for morning rounds. All day long I tried to convince myself that I was just too worked up about my patient, Noelia. *That's why I had the nightmare*, I thought.

41

A Bad Feeling

I was seeing patients in the outpatient clinic when Noelia Rodriguez came to mind. It had been more than a week since I last saw her in the ER. I had a bad feeling all day, but didn't know why. I walked up to the clerk behind the nurse's station.

"Janet, may I ask you a favor?" I said.

"Sure, Dr. Tavarez. What can I help you with?" Janet said.

A reliable secretary, Janet had been working for the clinic for more than ten years. She knew every patient and family member who came through here. Not much taller than me, Janet was big-boned with dark brown skin and eyes. Her dark, curled locks of hair were slicked in place and her smooth complexion made her look younger than her actual age of forty.

"Could you check to see if a patient by the name of Noelia Rodriguez came in for a followup?" I asked as I looked over the nurse's station. Janet checked the computer.

"Nope, the last time she was seen was in the ER a week ago. She never came to the clinic," Janet said.

"Is there a phone number where I can contact her?" I asked.

"Nope, no phone," Janet said.

"What's her address?" I asked.

"She lives in the Montgomery projects on Montgomery Street," Janet said.

"I know where that is. Many of my kids from the rec center live there. Which apartment?" I asked.

Janet looked into my eyes and hesitated. She tilted her head to the side, her eyebrows furrowing and then releasing.

"Janet, what is her apartment number?" I asked again.

"It looks like she lives in apartment 7A," Janet said reluctantly. "It's dangerous over there, Dr. Tavarez."

"I need to know how she's doing," I said.

"Then write her a letter," Janet pleaded.

I nodded. "I'd rather see her in person."

~

At the end of my shift later that afternoon, I got into my beat-up 1977 Toyota Corolla and drove off to Montgomery Street. I parked on the street and locked my car. I was still wearing my scrubs. I walked past a group of guys sitting on top of a car. They stopped talking to each other and began whistling and staring at me. I walked as fast as I could without looking back at them. There were kids and adults everywhere just hanging out.

I entered Noelia's building and walked over to the elevator. I pushed the button and waited for it to open. I looked up and saw a sign that read "Out of Order." *Oh no*, I thought. I took the stairway and walked all the way up to the seventh floor. I knocked on the door of apartment 7A but there was no answer. A door open behind me and I turned around. A little boy who must have been about eight years old was standing there looking up at me.

"Do you know where Noelia is?" I asked the boy.

"She doesn't live there anymore," he said. "She moved to Puerto Rico with her mother."

"When?" I asked.

"Angel, who's there?" I heard someone yell from inside the boy's apartment. A woman came to the door with rollers in her hair and wet polish on her nails.

"What do you want?" She asked abruptly as she looked me up and down.

"I just asked your little boy if he knew where Noelia is," I said. "I need to see her."

"Don't you know?" the woman asked.

"Know what?"

"Noelia is dead!" she said. "She moved to Puerto Rico with her mother and killed herself."

I felt my stomach drop to my toes. "When?" I asked. "How? I just saw her a week ago."

"Two days ago." she explained. "Apparently, Noelia went to the hospital last week and claimed that she was raped. Noelia and her mom were both scared, so they decided to get out of here and move in with some family in Puerto Rico. Her mother called me yesterday and said that Noelia took a bunch of pills and committed suicide."

I felt anger wash over me. It broke my heart to learn that Noelia was dead and this woman's lack of sympathy was really getting to me. I took a deep breath and asked a few more questions.

"Do you know where in Puerto Rico? Did she leave an address? A phone number?" I asked.

"Hell no! They kept that a secret. No one knows," she said.

"Okay, thanks," I said. I looked at the boy and waved goodbye to him. He waved back as his mother stood there looking at me.

I held my hand against my chest as I ran down the stairs. My chin began to tremble and soon tears flooded my face. I could feel my knees weakening, so I slowed down a little. Upon approaching the ground level, I wiped my tears, picked up the pace, and walked quickly to my car. The cat callers were nowhere around. I jumped in my car, locked the door, and sped off.

I made it back to my apartment and sat on the living room floor. I crossed my arms and braced myself. I felt powerless. Noelia was dead and there was nothing I could do about it. I doubled over and collapsed on the floor, and cried out loud.

42

ER Calling

My phone rang in the middle of the night. When I looked at the clock, it was two a.m. I answered the phone and said hello. It was the ER calling. I was the resident on call and they wanted me to come in.

"I'll be right there," I said. *Damn it, I forgot my beeper at the hospital.*

I went into the bathroom and looked in the mirror. I noticed how swollen my eyes were from crying so much over the death of Noelia. I was still wearing my clothes from last night. I took them off and jumped in the shower. Tears came streaming down as the water from the shower hit my face. I got dressed, picked up my purse, grabbed my keys and quickly exited the building.

When I arrived at the hospital there were three ambulances and two police cars parked by the emergency room entrance. At least fifty people were waiting inside to be seen. The emergency room was in full mode again, with cases ranging from simple ailments like ear infections and minor injuries to heart attacks, motor vehicle accidents, stabbings, gunshot wounds, and all sorts of abuse. Walking as quickly as I could, I put my purse in one of the upper cabinets behind the nurses' station and reported to the nurse in charge, Judy.

"Hi, where do you want me to go first?" I asked.

"Hi, Dr. Tavarez. Please see the patient in room three. Possible domestic abuse," Judy said.

I glanced in the room before picking up the chart. A bruised, petite woman in her thirties sat on the exam table. A tall, husky man sat on a chair right next to the woman. I picked up the chart and read the triage notes. *Patient came to ER complaining of pain in right arm. Left eye swollen and bruised. Small amount of red nasal drainage noted.* The patient's name was Francheska Lucca.

"Good morning. How are you feeling, Ms. Lucca,? I said as I stepped into the room. Looking at the man, I added a polite "Good morning, sir" while containing my suspicions behind a smile.

"Hi," she said sadly and slowly looked away from me. She began to pick at her fingernail polish.

"What happened to you?" I asked.

Her face turned white and her lips began to tremble as she opened her mouth to speak.

"I, I..." she said before being cut off by her husband.

"She fell down the stairs," he said as he leaned back on his chair and crossed his arms. I noticed his nicely-groomed hair, linen trousers, Ralph Lauren shirt, and leather dress shoes. *A look that radiates superiority—ah, a professional,* I thought.

"Oh, okay," I said as I played dumb. Are you her husband?"

"Yes," he said.

"Mr. Lucca, I need to examine your wife. Could you please wait in the waiting room?" I asked.

"No, I'd rather wait here," he said.

"Sir, this is standard procedure. I have to examine her privately. It will only take a few minutes," I said politely.

Mr. Lucca got up, looked directly into my eyes, and pinched his lips together. He turned to his wife and stared her down as he pointed a finger at her. "I'll be back," he said.

I watched until Mr. Lucca made it down the hall. As soon as I saw him open the door leading to the waiting room, I went back into the room, closed the door, pulled the curtain shut, and began my assessment of Mrs. Lucca's injuries.

"Okay, Mrs. Lucca, I need to examine you," I said.

"Okay," she responded as she closed her eyes and took a deep breath.

I visually examined Mrs. Lucca under her hospital gown for injuries to the ribs, breasts, groin, upper arms, and other parts of the body covered by the gown. I noticed bruising on her abdomen, burn marks on her groin, and multiple injuries in various states of healing. The injuries did not seem consistent with a fall. I began documenting my physical findings.

Knowing that I now had concrete evidence of abuse, I approached Mrs. Lucca and shared my concerns with her.

"Mrs. Lucca, I am concerned that your injuries may have been caused by someone hurting you. I want you to know that many of the patients I see are dealing with abusive relationships. Some are too afraid or uncomfortable to bring it up themselves, so I routinely ask about it." I paused for a few seconds and watched Mrs. Lucca's reaction. Her eyes met mine as she tried to crack a smile. I smiled back.

"Okay, I have a list of questions to ask you. Here goes," I said.

"Are you in a relationship with a person who physically hurts or threatens you?"

"Yes," she said.

"Did someone cause these injuries? Was it your husband?"

"Yes, my husband beats me," she cried.

"Do you have children?"

"No, we've only been married for three weeks."

"Do you feel you are in danger?"

Mrs. Lucca nodded, covered her face, and cried hysterically.

"What does your husband do for a living?"

"He's an accountant."

"Has your husband ever forced you to have sex when you didn't want to?"

"Yes."

"Is it safe for you to go home?"

Mrs. Lucca shook her head, "No, but he'll kill me if he finds out that I told somebody about this. Please, please don't tell him."

I handed Mrs. Lucca some tissues and assisted her with wiping her tears. She took a deep breath as she tried to compose herself.

"Mrs. Lucca, you are not responsible for the abuse and you are not alone. Help is available. I'm not going to say anything to your husband. I am going to get you some information on domestic abuse. Wait here, okay?"

"Okay," she said.

"I do have to order some X-rays just to confirm that you don't have any broken bones, okay?" I said.

"Okay," she said.

I pulled the curtain slightly to leave the room. When I opened the door, I saw Mr. Lucca standing by the nurses' station. He walked right up to me.

"Can I go in now?" he asked.

"I need a few more minutes. Please wait in the waiting room. There are too many people out here," I said calmly.

Mr. Lucca glared at me. I noticed some reddening of his face. "Five minutes," he said. "I'll be back in five minutes."

I watched as he walked back to the waiting room. I walked behind the nurses' station and contacted Lauren Davis, the social worker on call. Fortunately, Lauren happened to be in the ER visiting another patient. After concluding her consultation with her patient, Lauren and I met in the nurses' station. We walked to Mrs. Lucca's room where I briefed Lauren on Mrs. Lucca's abusive relationship with her husband.

Lauren knew that Mr. Lucca was in the waiting room and that he would be returning shortly. Lauren didn't waste any time. She informed Mrs. Lucca about the women's center in

Jersey City for battered women. Lauren realized that it would be impossible for Mrs. Lucca to take home literature, so she gave her a hotline number to call for assistance. Mrs. Lucca nodded and promised to call the next day.

Lauren had already left when Mr. Lucca returned to the room. He looked at his wife and then at me.

"Are we done now?" he asked sarcastically.

"Oh, here comes the orderly. He's taking her for an X-ray now," I said.

"What the hell?" he muttered to himself.

Mrs. Lucca closed her eyes and braced herself as the orderly took her for X-rays. Mr. Lucca waited in the room for his wife to come back.

Meanwhile, I continued to see a few more patients in the ER. I was finishing an order on a patient when Mrs. Lucca returned. I called radiology for the results.

"No broken bones noted," reported the radiologist.

I picked up Mrs. Lucca's chart and went back to the room to give her the results.

"No broken bones," I said. Mrs. Lucca tried to smile but instead maintained her blank look. Her husband shook his head and muttered something under his breath.

I reviewed the discharge instructions with Mrs. Lucca. I asked her to please call us back within two days to let us know how she was doing. She verbalized understanding and promised to call me. A few minutes later a nurse entered the room. She had Mrs. Lucca sign the discharge instructions and helped her get dressed. The nurse assisted Mrs. Lucca onto a wheelchair and transported her to the discharge area. Mr. Lucca followed along.

I worked in the ER the entire morning seeing patients from all walks of life and treating all kinds of injuries. There were cuts, broken bones, and gunshot and stab wounds. I even saw two more cases of abuse. When my shift finally ended at three o'clock in the afternoon, I was exhausted. I went back to the resident's quarter, took a shower, and crashed on my bed. I slept the entire afternoon and right through the night.

~

A few days later, I received a call from Mrs. Lucca. She had called the hospital operator and the operator patched her call to me in the ER.

"I left him," she said. "I feel safe now."

"Are you in a shelter?" I asked.

"No, I'm with my sister. We are moving to another state, to a place where he will never find me," she said. "I wanted to thank you for your help. I should have left him a long time ago."

I asked, "Did you get a restraining order from the court? This will protect you if he comes after you or stalks you. You can then call the police and they'll arrest him. I'm just afraid that he might hurt you again if he finds you."

"No, I didn't. I don't think he'll come after me. My brother is a police officer and he is now aware of what my husband did to me. My brother feels like killing him, but I promised him that I will never go back to my husband."

"You should still get a restraining order. Anyway, take care of yourself," I said.

"Goodbye, Dr. Tavarez," she said. "Please be careful."

43

My Mission in Life

It was hot today. Sweat was pouring down my back as I jogged along the piers on Hoboken's waterfront. Every day the news people reported high temperatures—a heat wave, I'd heard one say. Although the blazing sun made me tired, I continued my Saturday morning run. Slowly, I came to a halt as I approached one of the piers. I felt the urgency to stop and admire the view. The Manhattan skyline was spectacular. I could see the shipyard, the Empire State Building, and, yes, those Twin Towers, the World Trade Center.

The Twin Towers were two of the tallest buildings in the world. I thought back to the time when Cristina and I took the Path train to lower Manhattan from Hoboken to tour the skyscrapers. We walked into the South Tower, which was the number two building. The North Tower was the first one built. A tour guide escorted us into the elevator and we rode all the way up to the 110th floor to an observation deck. There must have been hundreds of visitors there. And what a view! We could practically see all of lower Manhattan. It was amazing.

As I stood on the pier, I took a deep breath and marveled

at the beautiful view of the Hudson River. *I can't believe I was born across this river in that big city twenty-eight years ago,* I thought. I breathed deeply, taking in the aroma of fresh coffee drifting from the world's largest coffee factory, the Maxwell House Coffee plant, located on the pier near my apartment building. *Mmm... delicious...* I then picked up my pace again and continued my run.

I began to think about today as I ran up the Waterfront. Today was a special day. Mami and Papi had invited me over for dinner at their place. I could just imagine Mami's arroz con pollo. *I can't wait!* I thought. The taste of yellow rice and chicken mixed with olives and vegetables made my mouth water—not to mention Mami's delicious sofrito. *One day,* I thought, *I'll learn to cook as well as Mami.* Today I would be spending my evening with the three most important people in my life: Papi, Mami, and Bobby.

Upon approaching 11th Street and River Road, I made a quick left to run toward my apartment building on Hudson Street. As I made my turn, I noticed a guy running toward me. He looked over and smiled as he passed me. It freaked me out a little because his face looked familiar. *An older version of Efrain,* I thought. His hair was cut short and he was more muscular. *It couldn't be him,* I thought. *I am just imagining things.* I ignored him and continued my run right up to my apartment building. Over the years I had thought that I'd seen him occasionally, in a bodega or somewhere in Hoboken, but I was never certain.

I ran upstairs and opened the door. Whew! It was hot in there. I drank a glass of water. *Hmm, I never thought a glass of water could taste so good.* I was so thirsty. I jumped in the shower and got dressed. By this time it was 1 p.m. and I was ready to clean my apartment.

I blasted music, listening to Gloria Estefan's ballad "Anything for You." I picked up a cloth and some Pledge and began to wipe a thick film of dust off my dresser. I sang along with Gloria as I cleaned. I was so into the music and cleaning that I didn't even hear my phone ring. As soon as the song was over, I heard the beep of my answering machine. *I have a message,* I thought. I walked over to listen and at the push of the button, I heard my mother's voice. Mami had called to remind me to be at her place by five.

I finished my house chores and proceeded to get dressed. I put on a light, summery dress which fit me like a glove. I still had my nice, guitar-shaped figure. After combing my long, wavy brown hair, I applied a little mascara and lip gloss which was really all that I needed to look good. By this time it was four o'clock. I picked up my keys, walked outside, and got in my car.

The drive to my parents' house was only five minutes long. I could have walked there, but I decided to drive instead. After a few knocks on the door, Mami opened it at full swing.

"How's mi hija?" Mami asked as she gave me a big hug.

"Estoy bien, Mami," I replied, giving her a kiss on her cheek.

"Mi doctora, my doctor," Papi said as he kissed my forehead.

"Hi sis!" Bobby said as he stepped out from behind the door.

"Bobby! Hi!" I said, hugging him tightly. I hadn't seen Bobby in months. He looked very handsome with his dark, wavy hair combed back. And he was in great shape—very muscular.

As Mami and Papi prepared the table for dinner, Bobby went down to his car to get some drawings. I looked around my parents' small, one bedroom apartment. Only big enough for two people to cook, the galley kitchen was nice and clean, even after cooking a big meal. Mami never liked clutter. The dining area was right off the kitchen. A few steps to the left was the living area. The white walls and birch hardwood floors made the apartment look modern and bigger than it actually was.

I saw pictures on the walls of Bobby and me when we were little. I found myself small again, age five and back in Brooklyn. I began to think about all of my childhood friends, Miguel, Sara, Blanca, and Millie. *Where are you guys? How are you doing?* I wondered. Those were the good old days.

Cristina, Nadine, Lucy, and I had been best friends for years now. We were like sisters. I was so grateful to have met them back when I was fifteen years old, just thirteen years ago. We had always been very supportive of each other. I believed they felt the same way too, or at least that's what they'd said three weeks ago when we had a girls' night at my place. I thought back to that night.

"I'm so glad that we met and became good friends," Lucy said as she held her wine glass in her hand. Looking in the best shape ever, Lucy had a special glow about her. She seemed happy as she spoke proudly of her kids and her husband, Al.

"Me too!" Nadine agreed as she carefully picked up a few chips from the bowl on the coffee table. She hated to make a mess. As a matter of fact, Nadine had become obsessed with keeping her surroundings clean, even after having three kids. She must have washed her hands about ten times that night. At first I thought it was a nursing habit, but then I started to think it was more like an obsession. *Poor kids,* I thought.

Tall and beautiful, Cristina got up and held her wine glass in her hand. "Let's make a toast," she said. We all got up and held our wine glasses at waist level as Cristina gave her speech. "May we be friends forever. To our friendship!"

"To our friendship!" Nadine, Lucy, and I repeated as we all held our glasses high and clinked them together.

I smiled at the memory and returned to the present. Mami, Papi, and Bobby were smiling too as we sat around the dining room table enjoying my parents' delicious dinner. Mami's rice and chicken was superb as always. Papi had made his own special salad: lettuce and tomatoes sprinkled with olive oil and vinegar and just a little salt. He also made coquito, and it was better than ever with a touch of rum.

"Wait a minute. I thought you didn't like rum," I said after tasting the coquito.

"Well, not really. But since you and Bobby are all grown up I thought we could celebrate a little," Papi said as he winked at us. We all chuckled.

"Papi, how's work going at the paint factory?" I asked. Papi had been working at the company since we moved to Jersey from New York.

"Busy as always. A lot of work," he said, nodding his head.

With a head full of black hair and a few lines around his face, Papi looked as handsome as always. Mami was still working as a seamstress, but this time she was sewing T-shirts in a factory up the street. She never really liked to walk far and always wanted to get to places as quickly as possible. By now, Mami had gained a few extra pounds. She still had her beautiful creamy complexion, just like she did when I was a little girl, and she didn't have any wrinkles.

"That's good," Bobby and I said at the same time.

"Nina, I have to show you something," Bobby said as his face beamed. "Come to the window." I followed Bobby to the window in the living room. "Look," he opened the window and pointed to a car parked in the street.

"What? It's beautiful!" I said. A bright yellow corvette stood out more than any other car parked in the street. It was absolutely beautiful. I turned to Bobby and gave him a big hug. I was so proud of him.

"You can ride with me any time you want, Nina," Bobby said with a big smile.

We talked about everything: family, church, and work. Bobby even got up to show us his drawings of some buildings he designed for a client in New York City. *Impressive*, I thought.

After dinner we moved into the living room to watch TV. Bobby had already turned the channel to a baseball game. As I sat on the sofa next to Papi, I noticed a newspaper on the coffee table. Papi was still reading the Spanish New York newspaper *El Diario La Prensa*, even though he was living in Hoboken. *Some things never change*, I thought. I looked over to the corner of the living room and saw Papi's Spanish guitar leaning against the wall.

"Papi," I said as I looked into his eyes and quickly put my head on his shoulders. "Could you sing me a song? I haven't heard you sing in a while."

"Ay, Nina, my voice is not the same," he said with a sigh.

Papi had stopped playing with the band as soon as he moved to Jersey. Not wanting to travel to Brooklyn for rehearsals and gigs, he decided to end it. Occasionally Cheo, Felipe, and David would come over to Papi's house just to visit and play some music.

"Yes, it is. You are the best singer in the world," I said, staring into his eyes with a big smile on my face.

"Yeah, Papi, go ahead," Bobby said, supporting my request.

"Manuel, you might as well," Mami said, smiling. "She's not going to stop asking."

"All right," Papi said. He stood up, grabbed his guitar and sat on the edge of the sofa. He warmed up a little and began to play a few familiar tunes. *Wow*, I thought, *he still has it.*

"Papi sing, please!" I said as I folded my hands in front of me.

Papi began to sing "En Mi Viejo San Juan" and a few other

ballads that I absolutely loved. He was still a star.

After a few songs, Papi put down his guitar and walked to the kitchen for a glass of water.

"I'm so happy you came," Mami said as she looked at me and Bobby.

"I'm happy to be here," I said. "It's unusual for me to have a weekend off."

"Me too," Bobby said. "I'm also busy with work."

"Nina, don't you have a boyfriend?" Mami asked.

"No, Mami. I don't have time for a boyfriend." My mind wandered a little. I started thinking about a few nice looking guys at the hospital where I worked.

"How about you, Bobby?" Mami asked. "Do you have a girlfriend?"

"A few," Bobby said with a smirk on his face. "What can I say? Girls love me."

"So what are you going to do next, Nina?" Papi asked.

"What do you mean, Papi?" I asked.

"After you finish your residency, what will you do?" He asked. Everyone looked at me as they waited for my response.

"Well, I would like to stay at the hospital and continue to work in the emergency room," I said.

"Isn't it a little dangerous there? It's got to be stressful, too!" Mami asked.

"Yes, it's stressful, but I like it." I said. "It's challenging and I like helping and saving people's lives. I feel like I belong there, like it's my mission in life. I know it sounds weird, but that's how I feel."

"Well, we respect whatever decision you make, Nina. We pray that everything goes well for you," Mami said.

"But I will always worry," Papi said. "You are still my little girl." He grabbed my hand and kissed it. "And Bobby, you are still my little boy."

"We know," Bobby and I said, smiling.

I got up to help Mami wash the dishes while Papi and Bobby watched the baseball game. Before I knew it, hours had passed. It was now ten o'clock at night.

"Stay here tonight," Mami insisted. "Both of you."

"Si, stay," Papi said.

"I would like to, but I have to do a few things at home," I said. "I'll call you tomorrow."

"Yeah, me too," Bobby said. "I have to meet a client tomorrow morning anyway."

"On a Sunday?" Mami asked with a frown.

"Yes, it's the only day that he can make it," Bobby said as he kissed Mami on the forehead.

Bobby and I walked to the door and gave each other a big hug.

"I'll be back sometime next week," Bobby said as he looked at me.

"I don't know if I'll be around," I said. "I'm so busy at the hospital. Call me anyway."

After opening the door, Bobby walked over to Papi and gave him a big hug.

"See you next week," Bobby said. He slowly walked toward the door and waved goodbye to everyone.

"Dios te bendiga, hijo," Papi said as he made the sign of the cross.

Mami looked at me. She knew that I was ready to leave. "Okay, Nina. Dios te bendiga," she said as we kissed each other on the cheek.

I turned around and ran to my father for a hug, "Bendición, Papi."

"Dios te bendiga, hija," he said.

~

As I drove my car to my apartment on Hudson Street, I began to think about my mission in life. *What is my mission?* I asked myself. *Hmm, good question.* With that question still lingering, I arrived home, took a shower, and changed into comfy shorts and a tank top.

I walked over to my dresser, opened a drawer, and looked through my piles of notebooks. I picked one up and looked at the date on it: 1968. *Wow! Twenty years ago.* I laughed at my childish handwriting. I turned the pages and saw a picture that I'd sketched of my friend Gina with her two angels and a cross above her head. I sighed as I took a few moments to reflect upon Gina and my patient, Noelia.

I carefully placed the notebook back in the drawer and picked up a new one. I sat on my bed with the notebook on my lap and a pen in my hand. I propped a pillow behind my back and began to write:

My mission in life... is to survive so that I may help those in need, to guide those who need guidance, and to inspire others to live happier and more fulfilled lives.

This sounds good for now, I thought. I started thinking about my kids at the recreation center. *What more can I do for them?* I placed my hand on my chin and wondered about this question for a few moments. Suddenly I knew. Besides supporting them, going to their show-and-tells, and helping them with homework, there was something else that I could do.

I can start a little workshop at the rec center and teach those kids how to write their own stories and maybe even their own books just like I did in fifth grade. That would be cool! I wrote a few more notes in my notebook and placed it back in my drawer. Then I walked over to the corner of my room and kneeled in front of the crucifix on my wall. With my right hand I made the sign of the cross, "In the name of the Father, and of the Son, and of the Holy Spirit, Amen." I recited the Our Father prayer and thanked God for giving me a loving family and the strength to do what I did. I also thanked him for giving me a happy life.

Afterward, I got up, jumped into my bed, and looked under my pillow. There it was—the rosary that Papi had given me when I was just eight years old. I held it in my hand as I snuggled in my bed. By now it was getting close to midnight. I closed my eyes and began to have happy dreams.

Glossary

Adios: Goodbye

Apurate: Hurry up

Arroz con gandules: Rice with pigeon peas

Arroz con habichuelas : Rice and beans

Arroz con pollo: Rice with chicken

Ay Dios mío! Ayudala, por favor: Oh my God! Help her please

Ay Dios mío, que frio: Oh my God, it's cold

Ay, hija: Oh, daughter

Bendición: Blessing

Bien: Good

Bodega : A convenience store specializing in Hispanic groceries

Bueno: Good

Burrito Sabanero: Donkey from Savannah or desert or plain

Cabrón : One who consents to the adultery of his wife

Café Bustelo: A brand name Hispanic coffee

Café con leche: Coffee with milk

Caramba: Dammit

Carniceria: Meat department

Cómo está my hija?: How is my daughter?

Cómo estás: How are you?

Coquito: Creamy tropical coconut eggnog made with spices and white rum

Dios te bendiga, hija: God bless you, daughter

Doña: A Spanish title placed before a name to indicate respect, equivalent to Mrs. or Madam.

El cucharón: A big spoon typically used for stirring Spanish rice

El güiro: A Latin American percussion instrument made from a hollow gourd with a grooved or serrated surface, played by scraping with a stick or rod.

El pato: The homosexual

El Súper: The Super

En mi Viejo San Juan: In my old San Juan

Esa es una piojosa!: She is infested with lice!

Esta bien hija: That's fine, daughter

Estoy cansada: I am tired

Gracias: Thank you

Hija: Daughter

Hola, como están?: Hello, how are you?

Hola: Hello

Los Reyes: The Kings

Los Timbales: Shallow single-headed drums with metal casing

Mamá: Grandma

Mami: Mommy

Maracas: Rhumba shakers, a native instrument of Latin America

Me llamo : My name is

Me siento mal: I feel bad

Me voy!: I'm leaving

Mi doctora : My doctor (female)

Mi hija: My daughter

Mi hijo: My son

Navidad: Christmas

Nochebuena: Christmas Eve

Papi: Daddy

Pasteles: A Puerto Rican special occasion food made from green bananas stuffed with meats

Pendejo: Dummy; idiot; one pubic hair from male

Perdóname: Forgive me

Pernil asado: Roasted pork

Pero que lindos son : But look how cute they are

Que Buena es la noche Buena: Christmas Eve is good

Que pasa?: What's happening?

Que paso?: What happened?

Que, hija?: What, daughter?

Si: Yes

Si señor: Yes sir

Siempre: Always

Te quiero mucho: I love you a lot

Te vas otra vez?: You are leaving again?

Tembleque: Coconut pudding

Tia: Aunt

Tienes piojos: You have lice

Una carta: A letter

Vamonos: Let's go

Ya, ya no llores: Don't cry

Reader's Group Questions
& Discussion Topics

1. How would you describe Nina's self-image when she was growing up in Brooklyn? How would you describe it at the end of the story?

2. Why didn't Nina tell her friends about her strange encounter when she went outside to play? Why didn't she tell her parents?

3. What did Beatrice, Daniel's mother, mean when she said that her son was violated?

4. How did Nina's parents improvise during Christmas? What did Nina love the most about Christmas?

5. Nina seemed to be passionate about her family. Who would you say Nina loved the most, and why?

6. Nina rationalized her fight with Sonia by saying that it *was an act of survival.* What did she mean by that? At the end of the story, Nina said that her mission in life was to *survive…* Compare both scenarios. How are they similar and how are they different?

7. How would you interpret Brianna's behavior when she told Nina about her relationship with Charlie? Was Brianna a victim or perpetrator?

8. From the beginning of their relationship, Nina seemed very cautious of Efrain. Why? What sorts of psychological issues will Nina endure because of her traumatic

experience with Efrain? How do you think she will over-
come these issues?

9. What was Nina's motivating factor for becoming a doctor?

10. Nina said that she tried to contain herself when she met
    Mr. Lucca. What did she mean by that?

11. Faith seemed to be important to Nina. How would Nina's
    life be different if she did not rely on religion?

12. What is the significance of the novel's title, *A Girl Named
    Nina*? What is so special about Nina?

13. How do you think Nina's life will end up? What would you
    most like to see for her?

National Hotline
Contact Information

As a courtesy, the author has included a few national hotline numbers for reporting abuse:

Child Abuse
Call the Childhelp National Child Abuse Hotline at 1-800-4-A-CHILD (1-800-422-4453). The hotline is available 24 hours a day and all calls are anonymous. For more information on the hotline, visit www.childhelp.org/hotline.

Domestic Violence
Call your local hotline, and/or call the National Domestic Violence Hotline at 1–800–799–SAFE (7233) or TTY 1–800–787–3224, visit www.thehotline.org/get-help.

Sexual Predators and Missing Children
Suspected child sexual exploitation or missing children may also be reported to the National Center for Missing and Exploited Children, an Operation Predator partner, at 1-800-843-5678 or www.cybertipline.com. You can help by reporting suspected abuse or by providing tips regarding fugitives and unknown suspects.

Rape

Call the National Sexual Assault Hotline at 1-800-656-HOPE (4673) or visit www.rainn.org.

Bullying

Call the LIFELINE at 1-800-273-TALK (8255) or visit www.stopbullying.gov.

Suicide

Call the National Suicide Prevention Hotline 24/7 crisis hotline at 1-800-273-8255 or visit www.niot.org.

About the Author

Norma Tamayo was born and raised in New York City. She is of Puerto Rican descent and is bilingual in English and Spanish. As a transient child herself, Norma spent most of her childhood years living in apartment buildings in Brooklyn and later in Jersey City and Hoboken.

A playwright, Norma directed high school students as they performed in her stage play, *Enough is Enough, Stop Teen Violence*. She made her acting debut in *Stand and Deliver* at the Genesius Theatre in Reading, Pennsylvania.

Norma worked at The Reading Hospital for a number of years as a registered nurse. She is a nationally certified and licensed massage therapist. She currently teaches the Health Medical Professions program at Reading Muhlenberg CTC, where she works with high school students.

As the advisor of her HOSA Freedom Chapter, Norma earned the Outstanding HOSA Advisor award in 2008 at State and National levels. Her chapter has received the Outstanding Newsletter and Outstanding HOSA Chapter award for more than six consecutive years.

Norma resides in Reading, Pennsylvania with her loving family.

CPSIA information can be obtained
at www.ICGtesting.com
Printed in the USA
BVOW08s0958020217
475011BV00005B/2/P